A NOVEL

Michael Heslin

A Skaty-Eight book

Designed and distributed by Bublish, Inc.

ISBN: 978-1-647045-29-6 (paperback)
ISBN: 978-1-647045-28-9 (eBook)

M ax and Salome, mother and daughter, lived in the hardware store loft. It was beside the New York Central viaduct. The north wall of the loft was the de Kooning fresco. It was known as the Dutch Boy fresco, suffused with yellow, orange and pink. It went to the ceiling because de Kooning had used a stepladder. (Somewhat unsteadily; he was, as they say, feeling no pain at the time.) He was not tall and had a soft voice. He was pale. Max called him the Dutchman though Salome never knew him. Back then, you see, there were often opened cans of paint in the loft that were available to all comers.

Another de Kooning, not as large and without a nickname, was over the double bed. That was the Tenth Avenue side and the partial sunset. This was unframed canvas, charcoaled in one corner from a small fire Max ignited while lighting a Marlboro with a candle. That was where she read, squinting, with a reading lamp. On a cloudy day there were many shadows and small things easily became misplaced by the nearsighted. It was inconvenient light but then you did not see the dust. There were green extension cords plugged into the four ceiling fixtures. The cords ran along the floor and along the walls. The floor was unchinked oak planks that had come from another building elsewhere in Manhattan long before.

Because it was a loft there were no rooms except the water closet. (Max long hoped to buy an armoire she saw in an antique store window on University Place but never could. It was in the window for years and she came to know it very well. One day without warning it was gone.)

There were no partitions either, only the restaurant racks from the Ninth Avenue steak house. The family that owned the Homestead liked Max, she had worked there one winter, and gave her old equipment. There were ash trays and dishes and silverware from the dining room. She kept her books and record albums (all found or bought used) on the restaurant racks. One shelf held her typewriter and she typed standing up. There was a ream of type-writer paper and a stapler and her pens and carbons. On that same rack were the coffee cans. Max collected them from the painters she knew. (She long remembered which came from whom.)

Some contained dried flowers but most were empty. You could not tell the coffee names except Lord Calvert and another that was clearly Savarin. Those two were not completely covered with paint drippings. One coffee can held matchbooks.

The restaurant racks were under the skylight. That was the brightest part of the loft and the reason Max had put them there.

The light switch was by the entrance door. It flickered the four overhead fixtures on. (They went off all at once.) The door was wood with sheet metal tacked to it. That was fireproofing to an extent. There was a fire extinguisher attached to the wall that was rusty and the rubber tube was cracked. When Salome was little, a spider lived behind the fire extinguisher and though she tried not to she could not help looking for it. She thought it looked back at her. Rothko worked on the door one night. He said he liked the surface but there was an argument and he didn't finish.

The arguments were too good to pass up, concerning as they did subjects that were never settled. The arguments could be very loud and sometimes stopped only when the train came through. If the train was heavily laden the walls and floor shook. There was usually a little soot in the air. If you were only there for a party (or to stay overnight) the noise was startling, something like a jackhammer, though not as frequent of course as the Third Avenue El. Salome and her mother could sleep through the train but they knew its hours. They knew its predictable ways and its rhythm. Salome was afraid of lightning and thunder and dogs but did not mind the train.

The door to the toilet was de Kooning on the inside. The door was paneled so the surface was uneven. Max said it was a study for the Woman series. That did not mean much to Salome and when she was older she did not remember what it meant at all. The Dutchman was struggling, her mother said. It was only a head but Salome was frightened by it. When she was on the toilet she kept the door open. She did not like to be closed in by the woman's head with the terrible eyes and teeth. The toilet had a wooden highboy tank. In the summer it dripped on her neck and the drops slid under her shift.

"Close the door please," her mother said, patiently, "no one wants to see you do your business in there."

She'd close the door and close her eyes but she could still feel the woman's face. There were instances when she waited for her mother to go out. Then she used the toilet with the door open. She gave herself stomach cramps inside but eventually the head on the door ceased to bother her. She was thinking about other occurrences instead. She heard the section hands, the gandy dancers, shouting on the track. Their voices came through the vent and sometimes they said things that greatly confused her.

The outside of the door was Franz. He was the only one of the men her mother called by his first name. The women she called by their first names too. She liked Franz. It said so in her scrapbook. He worked within the three door panels. Possibly the three panels were done on separate nights. There was a good deal of drinking then, seemingly of a desperate kind, and things do get mixed up in memory. (When someone brought a bottle it was likely to be open and partially consumed.) The toilet door was white and the middle panel had black strokes that looked oriental to some people.

When Salome was in her bed that middle panel was at eye level across from her and she liked to stare at it. Her mother was tempted to put a hook somewhere on that door. In the winter the loft was usually very cold. There was one radiator that was taller than Salome until she was in the sixth grade. She and her mother wore their bathrobes over their street clothes all winter. If there was snow on the roof they wore their overcoats.

A hook would have been helpful to hang your bathrobe on when you used the toilet so you could put it right back on when you were finished. No decision was ever made about the hook. Someone might have objected though by that time the parties were over and there was no one who would have said a word about it. Salome did not mind sleeping in her socks and when it was very cold she slept in her mother's bed and her mother sang lullabies she made up or hummed a bit of bebop like "Night in Tunisia".

"I'm here, darling, I'm here beside you."

The Motherwell wall was on the same side as the entrance door. The bottom half was blocked by the electric refrigerator and the stove. Salome did not remember when you could see all of it. When her mother first lived in the loft there was a small icebox. There was an ice warehouse on Washington Street and the ice wagon made stops. Her mother ran down to see the horse as much as to ask for ice. When Mr. Zwerling in the hardware store got a new refrigerator he gave Salome's mother his old one. Mr. Zwerling's colored man Emmett carried it upstairs.

After Salome arrived Mr. Zwerling gave her a stove. Before that her mother had used a hot plate though mostly she ate at coffee shops and cafeterias. (She ran a tab at the Square Meal.) There was a stub in the wall because the lighting had once been gas. That determined where the kitchen would be so the Motherwell, which her mother was of two minds about, was partially covered.

The slop sink was there too, which Motherwell had worked around. The sink was soapstone and had the same craquelure, her mother said, as old paintings. (Craquelure was not an easy word for Salome.) That was their water. Max picked up showers and baths here and there. She was an old hand at that. Salome was washed in the sink and then later she stood in a tin tub while her mother sluiced her from the sink. She enjoyed that though they did not do it as often in the winter. The old icebox was moved. It was her mother's nightstand beside her bed. Her reading lamp was on it and her cigarettes and the alarm clock she didn't like winding. When she had a present for Salome she hid it in the icebox. Salome pretended to look at other places and went everywhere in the loft while her mother laughed.

"You're warm, you're getting warmer, you're hot, you're boiling."

Sometimes it was a jelly doughnut, sometimes crayons and a coloring book. Once it was Venus pencils that Salome loved to sharpen. (She secretly ate the shavings.)

Originally the wall on the viaduct side was not plastered from the entrance door to the toilet. Mr. Zwerling's father had never got around to it. (One of the painters, more of a hanger-on than anything else, had plans to do that and then distemper it. He had big plans. He borrowed money instead.) There were no windows on that wall and the iron ladder to the roof hatchway split it in half. In warm weather they kept the hatchway open and used a wood framed screen to keep insects and some of the train cinders out.

The last summer Max spent in Provincetown, Emmett plastered the wall on several Saturdays when the hardware store was closed for the sabbath. Emmett was a highly skilled plasterer;

as good, Mr. Zwerling said, as any Italian you care to mention. His preference was to work alone with his root beer and his portable radio and to say he was fastidious was not to say enough. Emmett was mute from a childhood incident about which Mr. Zwerling junior was ignorant. Whatever the authorities at the foundling home told Mr. Zwerling senior remained undisclosed to others. The two boys grew up together and were anticipatory of one another's pleasures and crankiness.

When Max came back from Provincetown she was very brown and was carrying Salome. The freshly plastered wall delighted her. (Whatever Emmett did delighted her and made her smile. As Emmett was voiceless he did not complain or boast. This was a great relief after a summer with painters and writers.) She had morning sickness but looking at the spotless wall was nearly an antidote. The wall did not remain spotless.

She was at the club, permitted to attend as a sometimes girlfriend. It had reassembled after the summer break. There was a lecture and some popcorn. She mentioned the newly plastered wall to Lee.

"Maybe," she said, "I can scrounge a sofa to put in front of it."

It was the baby churning like butter, she supposed, making her feel this way. Pollock was standing there, shifting his weight from one ranch hand leg to another. (Max thought he was like a movie cowpoke at times.) After the lecture everyone went around to the Cedar to drink but Pollock was not there. Lee asked where he was but no one knew.

Max walked home, across the sleepy Village, when the bars closed. She lived far away from all the others. At four in the morning the meat packers were at work around and under the viaduct. Climbing the back stairs she saw her light was on. Pollock was there. He'd found the whiskey and had opened the gallons of house paint she kept by the sink. The oil paint he had flung and applied with his hands to the plastered wall was thickening into verdant valleys and hillsides. He'd covered the floor with the sheets from her bed. They were sticky. He took the Lucky Strike from his mouth and wedged it into a lower swirl to sign the wall. There were several other butts too. After that he collapsed on her bare mattress.

Max went out to the Square Meal and drank coffee with Alphonse, the son of the owner, and two butchers. (They were talking about Eisenhower. No one talked about Eisenhower in Provincetown.) When she came home Pollock was gone. A little later Emmett came in to see if his wall had dried properly. He blinked and left. Mr. Zwerling came by next. He had the knack of reading Emmett's mind because in many respects they were twins. Mr. Zwerling still called her Miss Max then.

"Miss Max," he said, "Emmett thinks maybe you should start locking your door at night."

If You Should Go Back To Your Nowhere

1942

T he man with the Ford business coupe was on the porch. The 7-Up sign was behind him. It was a Saturday morning, as wet as the day before had been. Another man, lanky in patched overalls, looked up with his toothpick. "I hear you got smokes to give away."

The salesman looked down. "You own a store?"

"Not exactly but I..."

"Then I don't exactly have anything to give away."

The lanky man was undaunted; factory rolled smokes were worth another try. He got up and stood beside the salesman. "You got anything against the Germans? Not me. The Japs maybe but I never met one yet."

As this met with silence the lanky man tried again: "I wouldn't give you a dime for Roosevelt. He ain't never been for the working man."

"How would you know?"

A girl walked out of the store. She had a carpet bag and a bottle of Royal Crown. The salesman saw her inside emptying coins from a sock onto the counter. She'd asked for paper money. She stepped off the porch and stopped to put a straw in her drink. The salesman looked at the back of her dress. It was missing a button. The girl walked on, swinging her carpet bag but not her hips. The carpet bag was threadbare and did not seem heavy. The lanky man waited until she was out of earshot. It was a good excuse to get close and talk low.

"Town tramp," he said. "I hear she is pulling out. About time too I say. Easy does it if you know what I mean." He licked his lips. "A tip like this is good for a fellow like you, don't you think? Should be worth something. That's what I think."

"Can't say I care what you think."

The salesman stepped down and went to the Ford. He traveled for Philip Morris and had a large territory. He was alone a good deal and lived many days on hamburgers and coffee. He left the town, there was not much to it, and came up behind the girl. The rain was sporadic. He braked beside her and asked her to get in. She did not question it. He asked where she was going and she did not question that either.

"When I get to Goshen I can figure it out," she said. "I'm heading for New York."

He knew the area but did not know anyone in it to speak of. "I can take you to Elkhart," he said. "Won't be out of my way."

"That's the main line stop up there. I want the bus."

"I like trains myself," he said. "Let's see what we can do."

In a mile or so he turned onto US 33 and went south. She said her name was Max when he asked. "As in Maxine? I have a Maxine on my mother's side."

"Just Max," she said. "It isn't short for anything."

He lit a cigarette. She took the pack when he offered it. She shook a cigarette out and looked it over. "These are tipped. That's for girls, isn't it?"

He nodded. "That's my problem with them." They were Marlboros. "Women in the city will smoke them. Not out this way so much."

"You like being a drummer?"

"Don't mind it." He did not care to talk about himself. The salesman stories he told on his circuit were mostly made up. They accomplished the same as what a real story would. "You leaving folks behind?"

"It wouldn't matter if I was."

He accepted that some people will not say more than they need to. When they reached Elkhart he parked at the station. He went inside and bought her ticket. When he came out she was beside the Ford finishing her Royal Crown. "Your train is in an hour," he said, "you'll get in tomorrow pretty early."

He had fifty cent pieces in his coat pocket. He gave her those and some cigarettes. "You don't know me," she said, "how come you're like this?"

"Well, there's a war on." You heard that every day and would for some time. "Now have something in the cafe before you go."

It was raining harder. "Thank you," she said.

"Don't come back."

It was the first time he'd seen her smile. "Can't," she said.

Once she was in the station the salesman backed the Ford around and returned north on US 33. It was the day before Easter and he would sleep in his union suit somewhere off the highway.

Max ate two fried eggs and toast in the cafe. She drank a milkshake. She bought *McCall's* and *Time* magazine at the newsstand. She had *The Great Gatsby* with the school library stamp on it. She supposed she could mail it back. This was her first ride on a train and the motion was pleasant like a rocking chair. At the Cleveland station she drank a coffee and bought another magazine. She liked to read. The conductor brought her a blanket.

"A bit nippy for April," the conductor said.

After that she slept for six hours. She woke up abruptly outside Albany. For a while she thought of the Mennonite boy whose parents had come to her uncle's house and called her names out of the Bible. They were harsh names like curse words. Her uncle was her mother's brother. Her mother was in the asylum and would not, her uncle said, see the light of day again. She knew that. She was sorry for her uncle. He had never been a success at anything and you could smell it on him.

There were soldiers on the train with baby faces. She looked out the window. She was pleased by the Hudson in the moonlight but the sensation that she would soon need to get off the train made her stomach uneasy. In Grand Central her legs felt weakened because she had been sitting so long. There were soldiers in all corners of the terminal. They sat on the staircases. She had never imagined such staircases as this train depot had. The morning papers arrived. A ship had been sunk in the South Pacific and hundreds of sailors were drowned. She knew about the telegrams that were sent out. They came from the Department of War.

The woman at Travelers Aid had a kind of uniform on. She was brisk and said it would be hard to find a room. I'm from Indiana, Max said, having a hunch the woman would understand. Illinois, the woman said, understanding. She wrote an address down.

"It is nothing special," she said.

Max listened and tried to retain the directions but it was noisy and she was sleepy again. She went outside and made the correct turn but felt undecided when she reached Fifth Avenue. The street lights were dimmed and there were many people on the sidewalk. There was a man with a tin hat and an armband who was finished for the night. There were no air raid wardens at home. He looked at the address.

"That's a good walk," he said.

She did not mind it. Her legs were hard and she was used to farm work. He pointed and she obeyed. She turned right at Thirty-First Street and followed the numbers to Eighth Avenue. The hotel entrance was dark but it was getting light out. They had one room on the top floor and she paid in advance for a week. It was eleven dollars, showers were two bits. She had seven paper dollars left, a silver dollar, and two of the fifty cent pieces. She fell asleep immediately in her clothing and did not dream at all that she remembered.

After sleeping three hours she went out to a cafeteria and had a boiled egg and rice pudding. Women went by wearing stockings and shoes with heels. She had a coffee and smoked a cigarette. A man asked if she would like his newspaper and he left it on her table. She looked at the want ads and went out to

Eighth Avenue where the traffic seemed insurmountable to her but not to others. She wondered if she would get used to it. By the end of the day she was waiting tables at a luncheonette. (The woman at the register added the checks up for her.) She smoked Marlboros until the end of her life.

1960

When Salome saw her mother at the typewriter she would ask who she was. Max wrote jazz and night-club reviews under different names. Only the New York *Post* paid her and it was not very much but the trips down to the newspaper office filled Salome with excitement. The trips began after a Friday when she came home in a silent mood from P.S. 11. Salome was missing a tooth on the left side, it was an upper tooth, and there were times when speaking quickly she whistled through it. In the schoolyard a boy laughed at her. They were playing tag.

"You're it," she said to him.

"Say it," he said to Salome, "don't spray it."

She was quiet after that. At home she was quiet too. She picked at her dinner though spaghetti was her favorite. Max was not indifferent to silence but she was not as disturbed by it as some are.

"I have an idea," she said. "The newspaper has money for me. We'll go together and we'll see what we see."

Salome didn't say anything but she secretly hoped it would be a great adventure. The next morning they walked to Eighth

Avenue. Max waved to men in rubber aprons as they passed them outside the meatpacking plants.

"Sometimes I take the subway," she said.

Today, however, they would take the bus and look at all the people on the sidewalk. Salome paid the driver and two dimes were returned to her, rattling into a metal dish. (She was small. She might have avoided the fare but her mother felt it was time she was fledged, insofar as the New York City Transit Authority was concerned.)

Salome could not sit facing forward. She had to kneel on her seat to look out the window, her knees smarting. As her mother promised, the streets were busy though not, her mother said, as busy as other days. When passengers stood up they pulled a cord and a bell rang. Salome was impatient to do that too though she could only reach the cord by standing on the seat. The last stop was Cortlandt Street. Salome pulled the cord though it was not strictly necessary.

They walked through the junk shops. There were stores with boxes of radio tubes and wiring. It was very different but on West Street she saw the elevated highway and the shine of the river. That was familiar. So they were still in the world where they lived. In a big building they waited outside a noisy room. A man came out and Max gave him what she had written. They went to another room that had windows like a bank. Her mother had a voucher from the week before. She signed a paper and was given money. Salome was not tall enough to see how much it was but her mother said thank you. They went back to the street and went under the highway to look at the Statue of Liberty.

For the New York *Post,* Max was known as Sweets Iberville, something she made up at the last minute. In her scrapbook where she pasted her clippings she wrote that it was more of an alias than a pen name. (She thought pen names were very interesting and was drawn to those who used them.) As she had no official standing at all she did not attend concerts. (For those she would need to buy a ticket.)

At the clubs Max was not charged because the doormen were happy to see her. (At some places they were more correctly bouncers but no one, she found, was as gracious to a woman on her own as a former prizefighter.) Her drink was usually Seagram's and club soda and the bartenders knew her limit was two and she never asked for more. She refused to take up a table or a seat at the bar. She stood where she could hear best and was not in the way. Max Roach, between sets, spoke to her at the Vanguard.

"You're the lady who stands," he said.

When she said her name was Max too he said it was a good name. He had given it to one of his daughters. Thereafter they smiled when they met. She thought the drumsticks floated in Max Roach's hands.

Max was easy to recognize in the simple black wrap dress she wore to nightclubs. It was silk and she was a bit hippy in it admittedly but that dress and her good shoes and a drop of the diminishing Jean Patou on her throat said she was going out. She also had a Schaparelli wool business suit she had acquired after the war by unconventional means. She did not wear it. The suit was clearly out of fashion but the material and tailoring were good and she enjoyed holding it up to the light.

As the loft did not have a closet, she stored the suit and other things for her and Salome in a steamer trunk. One day she found that moths had gotten at the business suit. Salome remembered seeing her mother hold the dress to her face without saying anything. She had never seen her mother cry yet and did not think she cried that time but she looked sad. The silk wrap dress was not in danger. Max washed it in the sink whenever she came home because it smelled strongly of cigarettes.

Some nights, generally a Saturday night, Max did not go back to the loft. She had never brought anyone there since Salome was an infant. If she did leave the club with someone she went where they lived or where they were staying. It had to be downtown. She did not want to be far off when she went home to Salome in the morning. It was no use for a man to say he was staying near Central Park and that the prospect, whether the voluptuous green of summer or a snowscape, was bewitching. She said no, politely, it was too far.

One man was hesitant. He was at the Earle on Waverly Place, he admitted, and it was a rundown place. She was happy with that. The truth was she had stayed at the Earle too several times in the days before she met Mr. Zwerling. She had no objection to old furniture and tattered rugs and the smell, it seems to be a smell, of senility, of age and decay. The Earle did not have good beds but they were not the worst by any means.

At daylight she was out, in her flats (her good shoes in a paper bag), over to Sixth Avenue and up Greenwich Avenue to the far west. On Tenth Avenue she'd stop at the Square Meal for coffee and a jelly doughnut to go. The doughnut was for Salome. Max enjoyed watching her daughter segment it like compass directions and scoop out the filling with a spoon and get confectionery sugar on her mouth. After that they had Salome's dreams to talk about and what they would do on their favorite day of the week. That day was Sunday.

One Saturday night Max was at Bon Soir on Eighth Street. The club had a piano trio and was very dark and smoky. It was not a jazz club and there were more evening dresses than other places. It was there she was given a martini. She spoke to a man at the bar who seemed uncomfortable. He said he was a salesman from Youngstown, Ohio and he was out to see some of the town. He asked Max if she was bohemian. She didn't think so.

"Perhaps they are like unicorns," she said, "much spoken of but much unseen."

He apologized and said he really didn't know what it meant. His hotel, the Roger Williams, was on Madison Avenue. (It was recommended by a man from Youngstown Steel, a fellow Kiwanis, who said they will not insult or rob you there.) She said it was too far. He said he was sorry, it was so nice talking to her. It was nice to talk when you were alone. She relented, supposing it would work out somehow. They took a taxi, something Max enjoyed as she never tired of the extravagance of red tail lights on a New York night. In the rain, of course, it was lovelier still.

In his room he became introverted and she understood he was not a man who often drank alcohol. He sat in a chair by the window in his shorts and undershirt and said again that he was sorry.

"We'll have a good night's sleep anyway," she said.

Max woke up at her usual time but felt she couldn't leave as quickly as she should have. The salesman reminded her of the man who bought her ticket on the Lake Shore Limited. That man had not demanded anything or accused her or berated her. It was getting to be many years in the past but she thought of him from time to time and that perhaps is all he would have asked of her.

The salesman from Youngstown had pictures of his two children and then he accidentally showed her one of his wife. Max stayed until nine o'clock and when she was dressed she made him laugh asking if he had a drop of cologne she could borrow. (He had Corn Huskers Lotion and she rubbed her upper arms with it.) She took his business card and set off at a run for home.

When Salome awakened, her mother was not there. She heard Emmett outside and opened the door to sit on the wooden landing. It was just below the roadbed of the viaduct. (Trains were rare on Sundays but not unheard of.) At the landing below was the entrance to Mr. Zwerling's apartment. Emmett lived behind the hardware store on the ground floor. He kept his step van in the yard. It was a white van with a snub nose and was operated standing up like a scooter. (The steering wheel was on the right.) It said Silvercup Bakeries on the side. When there was rain the dampened soot that fell from the viaduct stuck to the step van until Emmett came out with a mop and bucket. He looked up at Salome on the landing. His face was very expressive.

"Not home yet," she said.

The Silvercup van was not registered any longer and Emmett did not have a driver's license but he liked to go for short rides in the neighborhood. Sunday morning was best. He opened her side and Salome hurried down the steps and got in the cab. There was a peach crate she sat on. Emmett unlatched the palisade door to the sidewalk, stood behind the wheel, and tooted his horn that sounded like a kazoo. They rolled onto Fourteenth Street and turned left at Ticonderoga Poultry.

On Ninth Avenue they stopped at the Schenkel Dairy where Emmett bought half-pints of milk and orangeade in waxed containers, the kind Salome was given at school. They continued crosstown to Fourth Avenue and went south around Cooper Square to the Bowery.

Emmett stopped at bars and flophouses. Men without the price of a bed slept in doorways and in the gutter. They were rising to a further day, under a magnifying sun, of craving inexpensive wine and whiskey. A container of milk and orangeade was left beside each man. Salome looked across Emmett at their clothes and beards. An old man without teeth smiled at them. (She put her tongue up where her tooth was missing.)

It was a mild morning with a crescent of moon and the breeze ruffled the man's wispy hair. She did not believe he was ugly. When there were no more waxed containers Emmett continued down to Houston Street and then west to Tenth Avenue. Max was home when they got back. She had changed from her black dress, which she had already washed. Salome's jelly doughnut was on a plate and she sat down in front of it with a steak knife.

"I went on a magic carpet ride after work," Max said. "It was a very worn out magic carpet without any get up and go. That's why I'm late."

"I went riding with Emmett," Salome said.

"And did you say it?"

She shouted what her mother had taught her to shout when she was out with Emmett in the bread truck. "Hi-Yo Silvercup...Away..."

There were numberless mysteries in Max's scrapbooks her daughter passed over without comment. The business card of a man who sold plumbing parts in Youngstown, Ohio was one of them.

1985

L eaving the Salvation Army, Salome walked quickly. It was the third week in March and she was impatient. She was tired too because her sleep had been disturbed all week by sensations that George and Martha had arrived. She had only recently moved to her mother's bed. She was not used to the wider mattress without a protecting wall on one side. The first few mornings she awoke disoriented. The view of the loft was different from the double bed where her mother had slept.

Salome could see all of the large de Kooning when she opened her eyes. It was in a way inescapable. Trying to sleep, any unusual noise sat her up though she understood that ospreys would not come in the night. Their journey was long to this maternity on Tenth Avenue. Perhaps they came from as far away as South America though it might be only Florida. (Salome felt sure Florida was part of their country.) It did not matter as long as they returned to the home she had built for them.

The trains stopped running a few years before. It began gradually. She and Max hardly noticed at first and it was more the absence of gandy dancers tending the tracks and the noise of their ballast rakes and their whistling that struck them as different.

They had, and Max far earlier, incorporated the clamor of the passing trains into their lives. The cessation of human voices was more noticeable. One in particular, a man who sang aloud what sounded like church hymns, they slowly missed. Max assumed he was retired on his railroad pension and did not mourn the viaduct. She hoped so at least. As the walls did not shake so frantically or so often that fine coating of airborne dust was not as thick. In the busy days, before Christmas for example when Salome was small, the trains carrying turkeys and hams ran so often she wrote her name in the powder on her mother's typewriter. Max came and put her arms around her and hugged her closely and kissed her.

"You've signed it for me," she said, "it's yours now."

But unlike her mother, Salome never learned to type and had trouble changing the ribbon. If there was someone to write to she might have made more of an effort. She began once to type dear somebody but could not think of a name.

Mr. Zwerling remembered when the train first came through. He was a young boy then. It was something he could not forget because they demolished the house he lived in for the right of way. It happened to other buildings too. His father had built the frame house on a vacant lot next to the hardware store before Mr. Zwerling was born. There was a wooden porch and a pushcart out front. The older Mr. Zwerling had begun with a pushcart on the other side of town, on Eldridge Street, where life was densely crowded. There was more air on the West Side, though in those days the freight trains ran at grade level on Tenth and Eleventh Avenues. Mr. Zwerling liked to tell Salome about the cowboys.

"Sal," he said, "it was something."

They rode horses and wore ten gallon hats like in the pictures. The cowboy's job was to warn everyone to get away from the tracks when a train was coming. Mr. Zwerling knew a boy, he was a bit younger, who lost a foot to the train and died from the infection it caused. They heard him screaming. Mr. Zwerling did not like school. He helped his father and made deliveries. On the sly he did a little bootlegging.

"Bootlegging?"

Mr. Zwerling winked, his long wink that went on a few seconds. He'd stand outside the Homestead steak house and run that illegal errand for certain men he approached. There was a pharmacist on Horatio Street who made the stuff in his basement. He dispensed it in bottles that said Diabetes Cure on them.

"That was called hooch," Mr. Zwerling said.

Neither Mr. Zwerling nor Emmett were drinking men. Emmett liked pop of any kind, especially root beer, and Mr. Zwerling drank tea with lemon. That was all the stimulant, he said, a body requires. This bootlegging enterprise provided Mr. Zwerling with the pocket change he needed for candy as well as ornaments for girls on whom he had crushes. (These were many and thoroughly one-sided.)

He could not forget the day he came home and saw his father slumped in a kitchen chair with a piece of paper in his hand. It was a notice to quit their house because a train line was coming through very soon. His father rubbed his forehead with the heel of his hand. The right of way would miss the brick building the hardware store occupied.

"You're lucky," the older Mr. Zwerling was told, "you can keep that."

There was compensation but the hard times had begun and trade was poor. They moved to a rooming house on 16th Street. It was above a tavern that reopened when liquor was legal again. From the hardware store they watched the construction of the viaduct. It came down Tenth Avenue without mercy, like a marauder from the steppes. Mr. Zwerling was fascinated by it but his father swore in Russian and hit the anvil he kept behind the counter with a claw hammer. This helped to relieve his anger. When the trains began to run and they felt as if they and everything else would be shaken to bits, the anvil no longer helped.

The elder Mr. Zwerling put on his suit, coming back hours later with a foundling. This was Emmett. He was big for a foundling; the best guess made him six or so.

"This was not my decision," Mr. Zwerling's father said, "this comes from God."

When they discovered that Emmett really did not speak it hardly mattered. (The home said Emmett was quiet and undemanding. That was a significant understatement.) Mr. Zwerling was a little regretful but his father was not.

"There is too much talk in the world as it is," he said.

Salome stood on the roof. She hid her disappointment by the clothesline, taking down her sheets. It was breezy and it might be so the length of the Atlantic flyway. This would be George and Martha's third season. Like her mother, she enjoyed giving names to things. (But Max did not name the paintings in the loft except for the Dutch Boy de Kooning.) Salome had seen a newspaper photograph of a hawk living high on the Municipal Building. They said it caught mice in City Hall Park and stole a hot dog from a hot dog stand. As the grasses grew higher on the viaduct she thought of who could live there. She had a dream of keeping bees and rabbits, of fruit bearing trees.

In the Jefferson Market library she'd seen illustrated books about birds of prey and their travels up the seaboard. She saw a drawing of a stand built for osprey on Cape Cod. It sat upon a light tower in a high school football field. Perching posts were important so a parent could survey the skies for enemies. (Salome eventually added them, from 2 x 4's she lashed together.) She had a good start. The viaduct was thirty feet above the sidewalk. The librarian asked if this was special homework for school. Salome was not surprised; she very often seemed younger than she was to strangers. (She was not a great talker. She liked to be sure of someone before speaking to them and being spoken to.)

The platform needed to be strong for some birds will return year after year to the same breeding ground. The librarian looked at another book.

"The nest of bald eagles may weigh up to a ton after a generation of use," she said. "Those eagles stay together for life."

She asked if Salome hoped to catch a bald eagle. Salome shook her head. She did not want to catch anything. She wanted

a home for ospreys. This was in early May and when the platform was finished the season was too advanced to bring a mat-
ing pair to the viaduct. Late the next winter Salome climbed
to the roof every day. She looked south towards the water. One
afternoon they surprised her. (She'd been thinking of Max and
smiling.) She came up the ladder, her head just above the hatchway, and saw beaks and feathers and the construction of a nest
above Tenth Avenue.

Emmett built a duck blind on the roof for Salome. He did not
remember Tenth Avenue before the viaduct came. It was for him
a natural setting. It was becoming more so. (For Mr. Zwerling
the viaduct was a boundary, dividing his childhood, bootlegging
and carefree, from what came after.)

Emmett had a retentive memory and was a faithful exam-
iner of picture magazines. He gathered many of them on rambling walks up to Chelsea and down to the lower Village, select-
ing from garbage cans or sometimes finding old bundles of *Life*
or *The Saturday Evening Post* tied up with twine.

His shipshape room behind the store was decorated with
photographs cut from magazines. He was fond of ancient stat-
uary and cave paintings. Over the years he'd come to admire
and even love the Jackson Pollock in Max's loft. It could be he
dreamed about it. One day he brought up a *National Geographic*
to show Max. A rock carving from Indonesia was the same as
Pollock's handprint. Not long after, Emmett varnished the
Pollock wall. (Pollock was killed, driving like a mad fool in a con-
vertible. It was on the radio and Max closed her eyes in sadness
at the news. It was a lesson, presumably. There are corrals you

should not go near, she remembered, there are cars you should not get into.)

Emmett recalled pictures of hunters, the Chesapeake perhaps, hidden within duck blinds. When Salome began to construct her osprey stand on the viaduct in hope of attracting a breeding pair, Emmett chipped in. (As was his custom in most matters.) He assumed wild creatures like that would be particular in their neighbors. He built a box with lath and plywood, covered with netting and ailanthus branches. He cut down a stool that seated Salome comfortably at the spy hole. Still nimble, Emmett jumped from the parapet to the tracks and back. (Earlier, after the trains stopped running, he made a bridge for Salome with staging planks. It was three planks wide because he worried about her balance. She was given to falling at street level. That's my Sally girl with scraped knees, Max said.)

He looked back at the blind, judging how it would seem to migratory birds with insightful eyes. Lush meadows covered the railroad ties and the milkweed and black-eyed Susans Salome had planted were thriving. (As were the wooly dusty millers.) Otherwise this was Salome's territory, it's agronomy left to her. (But Emmett patrolled through the Nabisco Building, in search of makeshift encampments. He carried a crowbar. Having smelled human urine there he worried Salome could be surprised at night as she strolled along with her Coleman lantern.)

Emmett was not concerned about the women who worked below on the street. They were waiting for johns. He did not know if they could be comforted, if they could be saved. (They, like him, were the wind on the buffalo grass.) Their voices carried, shrilly insistent, beseeching the suburban cars like gulls. It was nothing new though there were more needles and glassine envelopes on the sidewalk in front of the hardware store. And across Tenth Avenue, at the old hotel, in the Sailor's Rest of past times, by the Cunard pier, the music thumped and echoed until early in the morning. Taxis brought men in leather jackets and blue jeans. The hotel roared like a mining camp as the city slept and when the lampposts went dark from neglect they were not repaired.

1946

After the war, when Max was living on Weehawken Street, she was unemployed more. Max had become accustomed to changing jobs, which were easier to find than places to live. She moved from one restaurant to another and had sales work in department stores. (For a while she demonstrated kitchen knives at Woolworth's but was not good at it. She ate potatoes with their skins as she could not peel them easily.)

When the soldiers came back she was working at an auto showroom on Columbus Circle. She was required to greet car shoppers and, the manager instructed, make them feel welcome. (How often in her life, she thought, she was enjoined to do this.)

She had a green Hattie Carnegie suit she bought on time when she was selling hats. There she was encouraged to say such things as: Madame, the cloche is perfection on you. A French intonation was preferred. (As well as the smack of a chef's kiss. Max didn't know what a chef's kiss was.) The owner of the hat store did not approve of her accent.

"My God," the woman said, "you sound like you're from Indiana, right out of the haystack."

Max could not reply to this. At the auto showroom, it was for Pontiacs, a salesman said he was sick of seeing her in the same outfit every day. He did not for long. The first man who applied took her job and he was permitted to wear his army uniform until he acquired civilian clothes.

There was an ad in the *Herald Tribune* seeking young women: *Girls wanted, must be five feet four, slim, attractive.* Max was sure she could pass all three. (Slim, of course, being relative.) She went to a building between Broadway and Eighth Avenue by the Minsky Theatre. There were fifteen women in the outer office when she arrived. Max had no seat until a man came out and told everyone to stand up. He dismissed half the women as too short. The man's name was Pincus and amongst other enterprises he contracted with nightclubs to provide cigarette girls. Pincus explained to Max that when a woman was below medium height the cigarette tray made her look dumpy.

"You don't have to be Veronica Lake," he said, "but dumpy is no good."

Pincus was not above hinting that he handled nightclubs such as the Rainbow Room and the Stork Club. After lunch when he was feeling effervescent he was likely to throw in El Morocco as well. This was not strictly true. Max asked what the position paid but was not heartened by his response.

"It depends," Pincus said.

So it turned out to be. Max was first sent to the Gladioli on Seventh Avenue where the tips were negligible and the long white pantaloons with matching sequined vests were itchy. (They were salvaged from a theatrical revue about a harem. It was a flop.) There was also a tiara involved. The Zanzibar was better but she was propositioned more and the natural proportion of being a cigarette girl soon was apparent. The greater the cover charge, she found, the more insincere one needed to be. She became tired of smiling and Pincus never provided shoes that fit. Still, she left him with regret. He made her laugh and never tried to rub up against her. (Unlike her cigar and cigarette clientele.) She noticed his advertisement in the paper until many of those nightclubs no longer existed.

While working at the auto showroom Max passed the Art Students League on 57th Street. Someone she'd met at Hattie Carnegie, her name was Margaret, said if she was ever desperate to try life modeling.

"You don't have to be a pin-up girl," Margaret said. (In the same sense that she did not have to be Veronica Lake or Rita Hayworth to sell Camels and chewing gum.)

Max looked into it and was shown examples of poses she would need to assume. She thought you stood upright or sat on a chair but there were recumbent and crouching poses she feared beyond her. You were not draped to any degree. (Max had understood procreation since childhood but nudity was another matter.)

"Modeling is not as easy as it looks," they said.

Max agreed and said she would think about it. A man standing at a filing cabinet followed her out and asked her to have coffee. She had not eaten that day and they went to the Child's by Carnegie Hall. (A discharged soldier was flipping pancakes in the window. This did not hold a crowd as it once had but it still made Max want pancakes. When someone else makes the pancakes they are better.)

This was Tony. He did chores at the Art League to pay for his courses. She was tempted to ask for a short stack of pancakes but he had invited her so she didn't. Tony lived downtown and had a studio on Weehawken Street. (Max changed hotels frequently and once dropped her carpet bag from the third floor to the street to avoid paying her bill when she left. She'd never heard of Weehawken Street.)

Tony told her he was not a painter as painting was finished, completely finished. He meant it was done, over, kaput, sayonara. (Tony liked to use more words than necessary if possible.) If you don't understand that, he said, you don't understand anything. He did assemblages, an expression she had not heard.

"I'm leaping the divide between representation and abstraction," he explained, "like nobody else can. Get me, sugar?"

Speaking of sugar, Max had never seen someone put so much in their coffee. He drank the milk in the small ceramic pitcher. They made a date to meet at the Waldorf cafeteria and he went back to the Art League. Max paid for their coffee. When she saw him at the cafeteria, the one on Eighth Street, he was with other people. She sat at a table nearby.

"She's a life model," Tony said, "very sought after."

There was more conversation than Max could follow. It was not all grumbling but much of it was. When Tony got up to leave she followed him to Weehawken Street. It was one block long and his studio was near the Christopher Street side. He lived there too and as Max had her carpet bag with her she stayed when he told her to sit down. The couch had no springs and her bottom nearly hit the floor. The light was bad.

"Doesn't matter," Tony said, "I'm not a painter. Painting is sunk, at an end, up the creek, busted, arrivederci...."

They ate cold franks and beans from a can and drank Blatz beer. (There was a stove but no sauce pan.) The unemployment he got from the G.I. Bill was ending but he sometimes found welding work. That explained the small scars on his arms and Max decided without thinking about it that he was more fun than many people she had met. (And handsome in a rough and ready way. Tony was some years ahead of Belmondo in the fetching, broken nose department. He'd boxed in the army.)

She did not know until later that Tony had two aspects. (Like a coin or a made up face when the makeup comes off.) When the enthusiastic phase stopped, the phase that made him run up a flight of stairs two steps at a time, the other phase ensued and it could be frightening. It was only a matter of chance that she met his good behavior first.

"I like bananas because they have appeal," Tony sang.

The Lilac chocolate shop was not far off on Christopher Street. They wanted someone for the cash register and the arithmetic involved was not too complicated for Max. It did not pay much but the chocolates were very good. She brought seconds and stale chocolate back to the studio and both she and Tony gained weight. They drank hot chocolate instead of coffee and ate root vegetables with chocolate mole sauce. Tony had been to Mexico and though he was not a painter the work of the muralists excited him. When they had a little money they bought enchiladas from the kitchen door of a restaurant on Houston Street and tamales from a sidewalk vendor.

Across Weehawken Street a man kept a stable with a horse and wagon. The man sold flowers in Sheridan Square and the horse, Peanuts, wore a hat trimmed with violets. Max brought it apples and carrots because she knew horses from home and she rubbed her cheek against its flank. The smell of the horse and the rough feel of its mane made her close to content. There were times when she smelled farm life in the wind. It might have come from as far as the prairie. She'd stop but then walked on. She had to.

On the days she did not work Max went out. It was noisy in the studio and the acetylene fumes made her sick. She'd walk to the Battery and come back up along the docks. (Or by Beach Street where the police mounts were stabled.) During the war the newspapers were forbidden to list Arrivals and Departures. When they began again, Max looked out for ships from the Cunard Line. She preferred the *Brittannic* and she followed its rise from the harbor surrounded by tugboats. Its berth was Pier 54. From under the highway she watched the taxis and private cars take away passengers amid the popping flashbulbs of the photographers. When the sailors came ashore she moved away. They were headed for the triangular hotel just above on Tenth Avenue.

There was a party on Ninth Street. Tony was one of the loudest and she saw that he should not drink hard stuff. There were two bottles of whiskey and he monopolized them. She hadn't wanted to go because Tony's studio had nothing in a general way and she couldn't iron her blouse. It didn't matter. The men and some of the women had paint on their clothing. There were at least two Europeans and she was a little breathless. Someone asked her if Tony was all right these days. There was a conversation about Cèzanne involving flatness and texture she enjoyed, though she was uncertain what these words meant.

She tried to look interested. There was no food and Max was sorry about that. They had not eaten since the day before. A man asked if she and Tony were involved. She could tell where Tony was. She could hear his voice from other rooms, sometimes shouting: "No...no...no, don't you see, you can't do that."

Max did not know whose apartment it was. At one point she collected empty glasses and washed them in the sink. Another woman began to help and they dried the glasses together. In the heat of the room Max inhaled the woman's perfume.

"It's called Cocktail Dry," the woman said; "I never wear anything else."

She came back with her handbag and took the stopper from a small bottle. She touched it to the hollow of Max's throat. "We can tell people we're sisters."

"Oh yes," Max said, "oh yes please."

Tony was having an argument and blocking the door to the toilet. He waved his arms. When Max went to him he did not seem to recognize her.

"Yeah yeah," he said, "in a minute for Chrissake."

When no one else would talk to him he gave in. He leaned on her shoulder going down the stairs and when they reached Weehawken Street her body was bruised on that side.

There was an incident at the Art League and they asked Tony not to come there any longer. He had shouted and pushed over someone's easel. He said it was not his doing, they were out to get him, but Max had begun to realize that is what he would say. It seemed that some things she saw as minor, perceived slights and inconveniences, enraged him while other issues such as the lack of money and eating regularly he ignored.

One morning, after several days of inactivity, Tony awoke eager to work. He said he was full of ideas and inspiration but the gas canister was empty. He threw his torch across the studio floor and banged his fists on the wall. He was nearly crying. When he was calmer he asked Max to go to the hardware store. There was an outstanding bill and he avoided Zwerling's for weeks though he had bought supplies there for some time. Max had not been in the hardware store and felt awkward asking for something without paying.

The proprietor did not appear to mind. He told his helper, whose name was Emmett, to bring a canister over in the van. "Ride along with him," Mr. Zwerling said, "Emmett likes company."

Emmett had a Coca-Cola chest full of root beer. He gave Max one and they rode south to Weehawken Street. Max recognized him for she sometimes watched the ships arrive when she did. There was a man at home in Indiana who did not speak and she knew the signs.

Emmett carried the gas canister up to the studio. He took the empty one away, looking around as little as possible. Over the next few weeks when Max was paid at the chocolate shop she put down a dollar or two on their bill at the hardware store. She began to stay for an hour or so and play hearts or casino with Mr. Zwerling at the counter. (She was a bad but enthusiastic card player.)

A butcher from P & P Meats (Primal and Prefabricated) brought his knives for sharpening. He relied on Emmett. The butcher looked at Max. When he came back for his knives he gave her a Porterhouse.

"Sear it in the pan," he said, "then under the broiler. Don't overcook it."

Mr. Zwerling gave her a frying pan. (Mr. Zwerling's love of cast iron was strong. It had been love at first sight.) That same day Tony had a welding job, repairing a storm door on Perry Street. He bought bread and onions and two quarts of beer. Max was cooking the steak when he got back. They laughed about the coincidence. She put the onions in with the steak. They ate it all with the bread and the juices ran down from their mouths onto the table.

"It's good," Max said.

Tony nodded. "It's been swell with you," he said, "real swell."

That night Tony was not restless as he often was. They were on the mattress talking and Tony said if he could make one sale, just one sale, they would be sitting pretty. He said they could get away from Weehawken Street. Max wasn't sure what to say about that. She liked it there more than anywhere she'd been.

There were other parties. At some of them Tony was subdued, at others he was disruptive. He seemed indifferent to her at times. (Painters, noticing this, began to circle. One held her against the wall with his hand. The whole technical power of painting, he said, depends on the recovery of innocence. A second painter, also interested, said that Ruskin stuff was all crap. They argued and Max slipped away to the kitchen.)

Tony's moods varied. One day he sent Max to Pearl Paint to find a shellac Mr. Zwerling did not have. (They pooled their coins because Pearl Paint would not give him credit.) Max liked Canal Street and delving in the junk stores. She thought the automobiles were louder on Canal than anywhere else. In the paint store a woman said hello to her.

"We missed you last night," she said.

Max understood they had not been invited. He needs to cool off, the woman said, but you're always welcome. When Thanksgiving came Tony went on a tear. He did not like holidays, they made him anxious and irrtiable. Max hoped to go to the parade; she hadn't had anyone to go with before. The man with the horse and cart gave her flowers he hadn't sold. They didn't work on Thanksgiving. (His joke was that Peanuts was in the union.)

She arranged the flowers around the studio and waited for Tony to come back. He'd gone out to rustle something for their dinner. He did not come back that day or on Friday. He had never done this. On Saturday she went to the police precinct on Charles Street. Tony had been arrested and was in the prison ward at Bellevue under observation. The night before he'd gone into the cafe at the Brevoort Hotel. When they would not serve him alcohol he began to take off his clothes. The police came and he hit one of them in the face with his elbow.

At the precinct the sergeant looked at Max's hand and asked if they were common law. He was being polite. Max didn't know what he meant. The sergeant said she would have no rights to see Tony as he was probably headed to the bughouse.

"Consider yourself lucky," the sergeant said.

You have to leave, the building owner told her. Tony had promised Max they were only two months behind in the studio rent. It was more than six months, the landlord said. He waited while she packed her carpet bag, staring at her body. She asked about Tony's equipment.

"That belongs to me now," the landlord said.

She went up to the hardware store. (She'd slipped the frying pan into her carpet bag.) Mr. Zwerling was reading the *New Yorker* with the Hiroshima story. The cover was coming off. It was three months old and had been passed from hand to hand.

"They have blown up the testaments," Mr. Zwerling thought, "old and new."

Max told Mr. Zwerling she might not see him for a while. When he asked what had happened she could not speak. (Like the man who had paid her way to New York, Mr. Zwerling was not overly given to interrogation.)

"Come with me," Mr. Zwerling said.

Around the corner Emmett was repainting ACTIVE DRIVEWAY on the sidewalk. He was also changing the oil on the delivery van and replacing a bicycle chain. Mr. Zwerling and Max walked through the palisade gate and up the wooden staircase to the first landing.

"That's me in there," he said.

They went up the last flight and into the loft. There was lumber on the floor and empty crates. The walls were bare.

"My father was planning to do something in here," Mr. Zwerling said, "but after they put the viaduct through he lost interest." He explained about the railroad right of way. "Months go by and I don't come up here. No reason to."

Emmett had intuitively climbed up behind them with a push broom and dustpan. He began sweeping. "There's some things we can do," Mr. Zwerling said. He turned and looked at Max. "Maybe you don't mind trains."

"I don't," Max said.

She dropped her carpet bag on the floor (the cast iron pan making a considerable clunk) and took the broom from Emmett. The two men left. She wiped grime from a window and looked down on Tenth Avenue. Max never lived anywhere else in New York from then on. In a few years she brought Salome there in her uterus.

1988

Salome never learned to roller skate. She was a little unco-ordinated and many of their streets were cobblestoned. At P. S. 11, they played monkey in the middle in the schoolyard. The boys roller skated around her and bumped her when they could.

"You got nappy hair," one girl said, "that's why you're always monkey."

She stayed away from school when she could. (Max did not finish any grade, her uncle kept her home to do chores. Max did not mind. The other children talked about her mother, saying she was nutty. There was nothing she could say to that. She was once asked if she was a retard too.)

The truant officer kept a record and told Salome's mother her daughter would not advance. Salome was left back twice and began years with classmates she did not know. It made little difference in the schoolyard. (The double dutch went on, every spring and fall. Salome watched from the fence, the jump rope spinning so quickly she could not hope to approach it.)

Salome preferred to be with Max who did not work every day. If the weather was cold or rainy their destination was the library on Leroy Street. It was warmer than the loft and the tables were the color of honey. Max read newspapers and then books. (When she was a girl there was a Bible, the Montgomery Ward catalog, and calendars in the house. The Farmers' Almanac was in her uncle's overalls. It never helped though he would tell Max a joke from it he found humorous.)

Salome looked at Beatrix Potter and any picture books with animals. She also liked the bathroom at the library, it smelled soapy, and the seasonal decorations the children's librarian put up around her busy desk. (There was a horn of plenty she wished would never be taken down.) Salome did not feel nervous there as she sometimes did in class. (Her teeth chattered and her knees knocked together.) She wet herself once and they made a show of disinfecting her seat and there was nowhere to hide. When Salome got her own library card and it had been laminated (Max providing the dime), the librarian congratulated her.

"I hope you'll continue to be a good customer," the woman said.

Salome promised she would. They were nice at the library and there was so much to look at. They took many books home, carrying them in Max's paper route bag. If Salome woke during the night she saw her mother reading and smoking by her bedside ice box. That was the best thing, to know she was there. It was easy to go to sleep again.

Some years after the train stopped running, a section of the viaduct was torn down. Mr. Zwerling heard it would all be destroyed, from Hudson Yards down to Bank Street, because it was an eyesore. As to that he could not say. An engineer the city hired came in the hardware store to use the telephone. (He had not been able to find a working payphone nearby.) Hoisted on a cherry picker, the engineer inspected the columns and arches and was very impressed.

"They're in great shape," he said, "a pity to see it all go to landfill."

Mr. Zwerling did not have an opinion. "If it happens," he said, "it happens."

He did not hate or love the train and if he lived to see its disappearance, as with the Ninth Avenue El, it would not matter to him. He had made his peace with the New York Central long before. Salome did not feel the same. The viaduct was to some extent her shadow, one she had lived beside all her life. (There was a storybook she took home from the library as a child. It was about a boy who became separated from his shadow and they both missed each other very much. It meant there was no sun above.)

The demolition began south of them. If you stood near the girders on Tenth Avenue you heard the earnest reverberation of the wrecking ball. Salome saw a feather float down from her osprey stand. The birds had left for their winter home and she had cleaned and aired the nest to keep the rats away. (When the osprey arrived in the spring she used the duck blind for a week and then slowly took up her own perch on the building wall. There were whistles and chirps of threat until they slowly accepted her as a temperate figment of sky.)

Salome mourned their departure but this was the beginning of her favorite season on the viaduct. She went far, deadheading and collecting, and watching the vagaries of light on the Manhattan water towers. She was on the tracks when she heard the first hammering and felt the rail joints shake. It froze her to the railway ties. There had been rumors.

Emmett on one of his outings had seen the heavy equipment assembled near the old Bell Telephone building. The viaduct was pulled down for several blocks and dump trucks hauled away the rubble. Each evening when Salome left the Salvation Army she expected to see they had reached Fourteenth Street. As it was they did not. They stopped at Gansevoort Street near the old pump house. There was no explanation except Mr. Zwerling's.

"Who knows, that's City Hall for you."

Salome was sorry for the tracks that were lost but happy for those that were ultimately preserved. In one respect the viaduct was hers alone. On the street, anywhere she went in the neighborhood, Salome followed her mother's steps. In her flat shoes, with her slightly stocky thighs and calves, Max was a walker. (She wore dungarees for these treks. They came from the army-navy store along with chambray work shirts that faded over time to periwinkle.)

When Salome was old enough, when she had grown into junior high and beyond, Max drafted her as traveling companion. Max did not want to hear about the subway. She liked to calculate the money they saved by walking both ways. (Max tried keeping loose change in a milk bottle or one of her paint smeared coffee cans. This never amounted to more than a dollar, the coins exchanged before long for cigarettes and Hershey bars.)

Salome learned not to lag behind though she never became as expert a jaywalker as her mother. They walked as if they might miss something up ahead, though what that might might be was never determined. Coming home was easier, less brisk, less uncompromising. They often finished at the Square Meal. Max had coffee and Salome a powdered jelly doughnut that her mother never failed to slice into delectable quarters if asked. Wherever Salome might go she knew her mother had preceded her at a distant time. There were other regions, in the great unexplored wilderness uptown for example, but these were further than the earthbound child could stray.

It was walking above that they did not share. Max's relationship with the viaduct was never so intimate. When the trains stopped running she was no longer moving about. (She might have enjoyed, as a kind of memory, the feel of grass against her bare ankles.) The viaduct was out there, on the other side of the east wall, not only unseen but now unheard by her. Max was never on it. So it was Salome's territory, a private reserve, separate from her knitted life with her mother.

A few days after the battering stopped, Salome went with her lantern to look at the cut. There was a barrier of logs, somewhat clumsy. (Emmett would have done a far better job.) The railroad supposed they were not keeping anyone from falling out or anyone from climbing in. Peering over into Gansevoort Street she saw how close she had come to losing the viaduct. She was thankful for its survival. The sidewalks were empty though further south on Washington Street there was dramatic activity and shouted voices. These voices were both gleeful and petulant. She turned her lantern off though she never expected to be seen. It was a brief excursion but a few days later it resulted in a dream that upset her.

When she was a girl nothing pleased Salome more than the hand cars the gandy dancers used. (After she understood that these gandy dancers were working men and not invaders. They were like the meat packers.) A hand car was special. If she was on the roof and heard its distinctive whirr and rattle she crouched onto the tar paper and peeked over the parapet. Two men pushed alternately up and down on the walking beam, propelling the hand car along the tracks. The hand car carried their tools, their shovels and rakes, and buckets of stone ballast. They passed her in a solemn way, the ceremony disturbed only by their unintelligible broken conversation.

Not long after seeing the cut, Salome dreamed she was riding the hand car. She was a passenger and saw the glittering lights of the city passing. (She'd seen stray cats like that.) The walking beam moved by itself and she began to feel the breeze on her face. They were going faster and sparks flew up from the rails. It became dark. Suddenly they flew from the Nabisco Building and beyond her house where ZWERLING was painted on the brick wall. It glowed brightly. She reached out but there was nothing to hold onto. They crossed Fourteenth Street as the viaduct shook underneath and pigeons flew from their roosts. There was nothing ahead but the end of the tracks as the hand car carried her through the barrier and down onto Gansevoort Street. She woke up with sweat on her forehead.

The following weeks Salome only went north on the viaduct. She worried she might have that dream again. When daylight savings ended it was nearly dusk after work. She hurried through dinner because a roller rink had opened at 18th Street. It was a nightclub too and there was a slight pulse from within the walls. A lighted sign at the entrance said Roxy. Looking down she saw the skaters arriving and heard their voices coming up to her. She enjoyed the laughter and she laughed also. It was like the schoolyard but she was not in it in any way. She was above it. (In the schoolyard the girls told her to sing Black Bugs Bleed Black Blood three times fast. She could not do it and she was pushed to the ground.)

She allowed herself an hour of it. All that young colorful life, all those boys and girls, was so thrilling. She wanted to wave to them but was afraid they would laugh at the girl on the viaduct who was hard to see in the dark. When the doors opened she heard the songs more clearly and the sweet sound of the fancy roller skates.

"You gotta have faith...faith...faith."

Not far from where she stood the field mice were thinking about the winter. There were more raccoons this year. They were great plunderers of the warehouse bays. (Nutmeg and peppermint kept them away from the osprey stand.) There were crows as well, so sleek and splendid. The bats were out, competing with swifts. Moles shuttered for the night and what might be a shrew scurried through the grass. (She had yet to see it up close.)

On her way back Salome picked a tumbled buttercup from the tracks. It was nearly dried. In the loft she looked through her mother's scrapbooks for an empty space. There weren't many for Max had tended her scrapbooks almost to bursting. Salome turned the pages slowly, adrift in her mother's life. She found a spot and with a dab of glue secured the buttercup beside a pamphlet from the Jane Street Gallery.

1962

Max was late for the first set. She hurried along Hudson Street in her tomboy shoes, getting damp again in the arm pits as she had been all day. This was the fourth year she'd delivered telephone books. She worked for Sidney who had a contract with New York Telephone. He covered 34th Street south, down the West Side, with four trucks he used the rest of the year moving office furniture.

"It makes for a nice break from the usual," Sidney explained.

This was his idea of a vacation, which otherwise he did not take. He laid off his movers for two weeks (who were very experienced and could carry a partners desk up five flights while debating Sonny Liston versus Floyd Patterson) and hired what he called stringers to run into apartment buildings with the White Pages and the Yellow Pages.

Running was the issue as Sidney did not believe in anyone resting on the job. The reason was simple. Work like this doesn't take brains, he insisted, so the least you can do is be quick. That said, he paid in cash and he paid promptly.

Sidney did not normally hire girls as there was the delicacy issue. (That is they sometimes fall down and cannot carry as much as a man though they are often smarter but that, as we have seen, is not an issue in this situation.) He made an exception for Max, he was not sure why. When she came back the second year he was almost pleased. (Sidney was not to any degree a man who was ever pleased.)

She was not a kid. Many of his stringers were college students who brought more brains than were necessary and he did not like to see anyone with a book in their back pocket as there was no time for that. Sidney put the same advertisement in the *World-Telegram* every year and received nearly the same results. When his new workers gathered for their first day at his office on Varick Street, Sidney gave what he thought of as his pep talk.

"This is the issue," he proclaimed, "you can't miss anybody. There are people in this town won't look at the directory once in ten years but if they don't get their telephone books like everybody else they got a beef and that beef you will hear through the rafters and I don't have time for that and neither does the American Telephone and Telegraph. All right?"

Sidney said American Telephone and Telegraph as opposed to New York Telephone or Bell Telephone as a way of impressing the gravity of the issue upon college students who were not ones to think about it. (As opposed to thinking about Cuba and attending Ban the Bomb rallies.) And if he noticed someone reading during his pep talk he asked them all to leave their books until further notice. In this way Sidney maintained an intellectually substantial library on a shelf by the water cooler.

He had *Being and Nothingness, The Power Elite, Patterns of Culture* and *Les Fleurs du Mal* amongst other titles. These books once got him a very nice piece of work with the New York University who were moving into a building they'd acquired on Washington Square. The man from the school saw Sidney's books and gave him the job without even asking for a bid.

"Any issues?"

Seemingly there were none. Because Max knew the ropes she did not listen to everything Sidney said. Well, she might know the ropes but did not necessarily know the situation.

"You don't know the situation," Sidney often said by way of good morning.

The office walls were covered with maps of lower Manhattan. Some dated to when New York was divided politically into wards. (They'd been left behind in a roll-top Sidney held in storage. He was fond of them, having grown up with the ward system.)

"No," he was heard to say, "that's in the Fourth Ward like always?"

The college students found this irrelevant. But Max liked the maps. They were warped and rumpled from years of humidity and radiator heat, a kind of aging akin to what gravity does. Sidney looked at Max not listening to him and vowed vengeance. He'd fix her wagon. Her first year he regretted immediately hiring a girl and put her on his truck to keep an eye on her.

"I've got my eye on you. You don't know the situation."

Max went up and down the truck ramp at a run and though she could not carry as many telephone books as the boys she went twice as fast. It made him suspicious.

"Possibly, maybe, I got an issue here," he said.

The second morning Max brought him a jelly doughnut. When she wasn't looking he poked it with the eraser end of his pencil. It seemed all right and he ate it with a cup of coffee that was less than two days old. (Sidney sometimes slept upstairs in a hammock slung between two pillars. He was surrounded by wooden moving barrels packed with excelsior. Sometimes he listened to the ballgame on the radio but most often read himself to sleep with the evening paper or *Being and Nothingness*.)

"What does it all mean?"

Consequently, Sidney was not bothered when Max applied in subsequent years. Not listening to his pep talk was unfortunate but he had to admit the work did not change considerably over time. (Sidney used a 1951 Manhattan directory as weathered as old slippers or a well used pipe. As he did not wear slippers or smoke a pipe the directory was just as comforting.) His lecture began with a few remarks as to the importance of telephone books; that they were, for instance, the lifeblood of a thriving metropolis and so forth.

"Breathes there a man with soul so dead," one of the college students intoned dramatically, "who has not looked up his name in the telephone book?"

The other students laughed. Sidney didn't get it but against his better judgment he recognized something of the existentialist viewpoint. It was times like this when it was relaxing to look at Max in her dungarees and faded work shirt. As far as Sidney knew Max never made fun of him. For that matter she didn't talk much. That was a plus as Sidney was prone to misunderstanding.

It was only after two years that he learned where Max lived. He bought rat traps and other merchandise from Zwerling's and enjoyed its monosyllabic atmosphere. (He especially liked Emmett who did not talk at all.) A man returned from shopping at Zwerling's undisturbed in mind. You couldn't say that about everywhere.

You surely could not say it anymore about Jos. Spivak & Son. Spivak was a colleague and competitor of Sidney's on Charlton Street. (In the Eighth Ward.) Spivak had recently gone residential at the urging of his smart alec son, Melvin. (Sidney conceded that a son to bring into the firm and carry on the name was nothing to sneeze at but don't be so pushy.)

Their companies had avoided residential moving, believing it to be an invitation to unnecessary aggravation. Invariably there are accusations of absent heirlooms and mementoes that bring on telephone calls, lawyer's letters, and reduced charges. (There is little sentimental about office furniture.) It was not worth the trouble. Wisenheimer Melvin (he preferred Mel) saw it differently.

Mel encouraged his father to expand and taking a page from Sidney's book hired college students who worked nights and weekends moving households. He advertised that his movers were young, smart, and respectful scholars who treat your valuables like their own. (There was a snappy ad in the *Voice* he had designed while burning the midnight oil, just like Karl Marx or Dostoyevsky. Mel planned to be mayor someday if not more than that.)

The last time Sidney stopped in Charlton Street to say hello he found the office occupied by young men listening to The Kingston Trio and reading. He recognized some of the books. The senior Spivak had escaped upstairs to get some quiet. He was sitting with a double-entry ledger beside his wooden moving barrels filled with excelsior.

"It's the writing on the wall," he said.

"That's an issue," Sidney agreed.

He wondered if the writing would soon be on his wall though whose writing it would be he could not say. Evidently, he did not know the situation. (Imagine, after all this time.)

On a Saturday it was the usual round. They were finishing up at London Terrace. It has so many apartments it is almost a day's work in itself and has the kind of tenants who like their telephone books clean and crisp or you will hear about it.

He realized he would not see Max again for another year and perhaps not even then the way things were going. That's how it was. He'd decided to give her a present but could not think of anything as it was out of his league. What to do, what to do? So he invented a sister.

"It's her birthday," he mumbled, "what's a good perfume?"

"I like Jean Patou," Max said.

Sidney went up to Fifth Avenue and bought a bottle. It was enjoyable and he was impressed with how carefully the woman at the perfume counter at Altman's wrapped the package. He wondered if she had any moving experience. Her hands did not look like it. On the last day when he paid Max off he gave her the perfume.

"I guess you got a birthday too," he said, mumbling again.

Sidney gave Max a lift home to Tenth Avenue. She opened the Jean Patou and put some on her throat and the cab of the truck was filled with it. He thought it was pretty nice.

"Tell that old Zwerling I said hiya and the colored kid too."

Mr. Zwerling was probably younger than Sidney but Max said she would. Mr. Zwerling was playing checkers with Salome and listening to Kennedy on the radio.

"These people will get us all killed dead some day," Mr. Zwerling said.

Max and Salome went upstairs and cuddled on the sofa for an hour under the Jackson Pollock. (The sofa came from the street. Max scoured the neighborhood on bulk pickup day for six months until she saw one she liked. She called the store from a phone booth and told Mr. Zwerling. When Emmett came with the Silvercup van, Max was sitting on the sofa debating with a woman who said she had seen it first. Max won.)

Max was tired and her legs were sore. She took two of her daughter's St. Joseph aspirins and got dressed to go out. She heated tomato soup and put out saltines though Salome would eat little of it. She knew where her mother was going and knew she would bring home real spaghetti that was just as good cold as it was hot.

Max put on her wrap dress but not her good shoes and opened the new bottle of Jean Patou for another drop under her chin. She carried her raincoat and did not begin to hurry until she reached Hudson Street. The raincoat was unnecessary and her dress was clinging to her back and shoulders. At Spring Street people were standing outside the Half Note. She went in and stood at the bar. Wynton Kelly was already playing. Max hung up her raincoat and when she came back there was a 7 & 7 beside an ashtray. She'd forgotten her cigarettes and borrowed a Viceroy from the bartender. Francesca came over to say there was a table for her. Max shook her head.

"I can see his hands from here."

Francesca knew that was her way. Max liked to see their hands. During the break she went to the cigarette machine and bought Marlboros. When she went back to the bar Alexis was coming out of the john. Alexis had a significant black eye. She took a Marlboro.

"I walked into a door," she said, "twice".

Max decided that was not funny. "Okay," she said.

"I didn't see you at the party."

"Oh well, you know."

The trio was setting up again and Max turned towards them. She did not want to talk about the Five Spot. She did not go to the closing night bash because she was sure Frank would be there. He would not have missed it. She felt foolish carrying a torch for a man who did not want women that way. For some years she had felt like this, since she had first seen him laughing, crammed in a booth with other people. That Irish face with the funny nose. He was telling a story about the navy and she tried to get closer to hear. He was friends with other women and seeing that made it harder. Max supposed she was not interesting enough. (She was on the border. When the canvas was stretched she was folded back onto the frame, out of the picture.) She often felt stupid.

She had difficulty thinking of things to say. I'm a walker, she wanted to tell Frank, not a talker. It did not sound smart. Once she told him about the loft, about the large and small de Koonings and the Franz Kline. He said he would come see them but time went by and she was too hesitant to mention them again. After a while she did not see many of his friends as she once had so the connection between them failed. She did stand in the back for a reading he gave but did not go up to him afterward. Now it was too late.

Alexis went back to her table. Max had a second 7 & 7 and ate some bread and butter and olives Francesca brought over. Max did not stay for the second set. She had enough to write about. A man stopped her as she was getting her raincoat.

"I've seen you in here before," he said.

Max smiled but said she was going home. She was tired and had seen Salome so little while she was delivering telephone books. She said goodnight to Francesca.

"For the little one," Francesca said.

Max left, holding her raincoat and the brown paper bag. She went uptown past the White Horse and the police station and then turned towards Tenth Avenue. Salome was asleep when she came in. Max undressed but did not get in her own bed. She got in beside her daughter and in her sleep Salome turned her body towards her mother. The first train went by at five o'clock. Max opened her eyes and then closed them again. Salome did not stir. The passing of the trains was resolved in her dreams.

"You came to me from out of nowhere," Max whispered, falling asleep again.

Later in the morning Salome had spaghetti and meatballs for breakfast while her mother was standing at the typewriter.

1949

M r. Zwerling was handy and liked tinkering. (Some of this had rubbed off from his father. Mr. Zwerling senior did general repairs and was paid for his time in broilers and fryers, bottles of seltzer, and other exchangeable goods.) A corner of the hardware store was given over to appliances to be mended or overhauled. (Rewiring a blender had brought considerable fulfillment.)

There were fewer neighbors than they once were but workers at the meat processing plants brought in vacuum cleaners, toasters, and broken dollhouses for Mr. Zwerling to examine when he had the chance. (He usually did.)

"I'll see what I can do." He liked what could be taken apart completely and reassembled. "You got to see the works to understand it. That's my motto."

When he was a boy Mr. Zwerling built crystal radios and telegraph keys. The telegraph keys were part of imagination and heroism. His father had watched the *Carpathia* dock when it brought the *Titanic* survivors to Pier 54. There were thousands of people lining Tenth Avenue. The crowd was so dense his father could not open the store or stand in the street. The elder Mr. Zwerling went up to the roof and watched as the stacks of the *Carpathia* became visible on the river. He was an onlooker. As the ship approached the pier Mr. Zwerling's father said there was a sound. It was neither joy nor sorrow, it was one long breath.

He himself had come on a sailing ship though all he remembered clearly was being poked in his bare chest by a very hard finger at Castle Clinton. By the time his son built his first telegraph key (when he was not bootlegging) the tide of immigrants had been corked and there was less need for a tireless wireless operator to receive signals of distress.

Mr. Zwerling was not religious but closed the store on Saturdays because his father had. Before the war, when the Ninth Avenue El was still running, he took the express south to Cortlandt Street, to Radio Row. He poked with other tinkering men at the crates of electronic detritus that protruded from the surrounding shops. There was minimal conversation and infrequent recognition of another's luck. He often saw the same faces though during the war all the men were old. (His cleft palate had deferred him from the army.)

At the hardware store Mr. Zwerling had buckets of switches, transformers and variable condensers he was planning to do something with. Emmett puckered his mouth at them, they were dust collectors. Yet when a faulty radio was dropped off and a part was found in a bucket Mr. Zwerling was triumphant.

"See?"

On his Saturdays, Emmett sometimes rode the IND to 155th Street and spent the afternoon at the American Indian museum. He did not otherwise use the subway. The museum was a quiet place that drew him back again and again. The totems and head-dresses, the fetishes and kachina dolls gave him great pleasure. On occasion Mr. Zwerling wondered if Emmett was Negro on both sides. There was something unheralded in Emmett's face, undamaged by speech, that reminded Mr. Zwerling of Joe Two-Axe.

Joe was an Oneida who had fallen out with his brethren in Brooklyn. He lived in rooming houses nearby and worked, when he felt like it, as a meat cutter at different plants in the neighborhood. His mailing address was Donahue's on West Street, a bar that looked more savage than it was if only due to patrons with blood stained aprons. Joe Two-Axe loved tools and could spend an hour in the hardware store admiring them. When he hefted a pick or a spiking maul his face flushed with enjoyment as he savored the grip.

"That's hickory," Mr. Zwerling said.

Joe Two-Axe had worked on skyscrapers and the Bayonne Bridge. During the dig for the IND tunnel, sandhogs came into Donahue's. They were soiled, blackened, their irises bright within dark caverns.

"Couldn't do that work," Joe Two-Axe said.

He could roll a cigarette standing on a girder sixty stories up but he would not go underground. When he was riveting on the Bayonne Bridge a wind gust nearly tossed him from a steel arch into the Kill Van Kull. This story chilled Emmett to the bone. Heights did not bother Emmett but he was afraid of the water.

Every December Joe hitchhiked north to the reservation with a heavy canvas sack. Because Zwerling's had a layaway policy he paid money on tools throughout the year. These were presents.

"Maybe I don't come back this time," he said.

He did come back. Because it was colder up there, he said. But Joe Two-Axe was argumentative with his own people and one thing led to another. (That's what makes exile, Mr. Zwerling said, lamenting a condition to be avoided at all costs.)

Sometimes when there was a pow-wow in Brooklyn Joe went. Some things, familiarity perhaps, left him cut off, detached, and he did not contribute. The Hoyt and Schermerhorn stop on the IND was not far from Tenth Avenue as the crow flies but it was sufficient for him. (Crows held a significant place in Joe's worldview. He honored them above all things.)

At Donahue's, Joe drank with Poles and Slovaks. They had fathers and brothers who worked on the killing floors uptown. (Others were dock-wallopers, along the entire Port of New York.) One of the bartenders called him chief. He got along with them. On paydays Joe left a few dollars on account at the hardware store before he spent it all. (Another day he dropped a kitten he called Butch on the counter. Mr. Zwerling and Emmett were initially dismayed but were won over to extent that Butch lived in the store for twenty-two years. Butch was a female.)

Emmett brought a pamphlet back from the Indian museum. It was about potlatch. Mr. Zwerling looked at it while he was cutting a piece of glass for a picture frame. (The picture was a truck driver's mother in the old country. It fell off the wall and the truck driver brought it in to fix.) Mr. Zwerling became so interested in the pamphlet he pricked his thumb with the point driver. Emmett took over and Mr. Zwerling stood by the window where the light was better and he could sit on a spool of bulk wire.

"Very interesting," he said. "These Indians out there have a feast and give everything away."

Emmett knew that already because he had read the pamphlet. Like his father, Mr. Zwerling was given to bursts of exposition.

"If they're doing good it shows how good they're doing. But it maybe means more than showing you're a big shot. It ties everything together for people because people forget. It could be a mitzvah; that's what I'm thinking."

Mr. Zwerling's father did not refuse any beggar. "It's a mitzvah," he said, "what can you do?"

On Saturdays during his son's childhood, Mr. Zwerling senior made treks to the East Side. This was ostensibly to attend services but actually to smoke a cigar in the sunshine and buy pickles. He passed his synagogue on Norfolk Street to be assured that it was still standing. (If it had not been standing he wouldn't, being Jewish, have been unduly shocked.) Then he went on a tour of any shops that were open on the sabbath. (He did not neglect the horseradish woman.) There were mendicants he often encountered to whom he distributed coins and half-sour pickles. Whatever pickles were left in the pail he ate with his family.

Emmett never developed a taste for pickles but in later years, bound home from a jaunt, he often brought Mr. Zwerling a pint of giardiniera from Tomarelli's on Ninth Avenue. Standing at the front door, Mr. Zwerling ate the pickled vegetables with his fingers and watched the traffic on Tenth Avenue. (Trucks were more frequent, a sign of things to come.) Again like his father, he was only nominal in his observances but he did maintain a private day of atonement.

He closed the store and fasted and asked forgiveness for his offenses. He knew of some and imagined others caught in their wake would be included also. His disfigurement had kept him tied to the store when he might have shipped out to sea or ridden the rails to California and become a movie stunt man. This was a lie and he asked forgiveness for believing it when he knew better. He did not return to it as he once did but there it was yet, like the alcohol another man could not resist, there within reach. It brought consolation but then it brought guilt and he was ashamed.

Mr. Zwerling did not wait until autumn to atone, for things pile up and an ancient calendar falls behind. When his father died he went into mourning and did not shave. He began to hope, it was nearly an ambition, that a mustache would cover the fissure on his mouth. He looked every day and the blasphemy was apparent. The mustache split more or less as his lip did and he appeared as a wild beast and a ferocious one at that. When the period of mourning was over Mr. Zwerling shaved and thought about atoning.

"God will not be mocked."

It was a warm July morning, a Saturday, and sultry inside the store with the doors and windows closed. Mr. Zwerling listened to Rambling With Gambling and the news. (Buckwheat coal was rising fifty cents a ton. One of the last jobs he did with his father was installing the mechanical stoker. You spend money to save money, his father said.)

He dusted the radio. (He had a great affection for bakelite, but it showed the dust.) He checked the time of the Giants game in the paper. It was five hours until then. Emmett had brought in the milk and butter and then gone out. If the mood was on him he would not be back until dark.

Mr. Zwerling unpacked a shipment of light bulbs and then went to the basement to work on cobwebs. (Emmett left spiders alone.) This raised a sweat. He came upstairs and dampened a handkerchief with vinegar and tied it around his neck. He went out back for some air. Emmett had not taken the step-van. When the old delivery truck gave out, they went to an auction in Hoboken. It was an expedition they both enjoyed. There was nothing like seeing new places. (Emmett did get a little seasick on the ferry.) When they saw the step-van in the lot Emmett was enthralled. It was not precisely what they required but deliveries were not what they once were. It said Silvercup on the side and there were bakery racks in the rear and a Silvercup Bakery cap stuffed in the wheelbase.

"That's the real McCoy," Mr. Zwerling had said.

Emmett proved reluctant to paint over Silvercup and Mr. Zwerling had given up asking. As Emmett did the driving it was his choice. A driver's license was another matter. Emmett came with a birth certificate. Mr. Zwerling kept it with his other family papers in a metal box upstairs. Emmett's birth certificate was stamped ILLEGITIMATE. The box was stored on a shelf with a menorah and a lacquered tea set his mother had treasured. Mr. Zwerling kept the metal box locked. That birth certificate was their concern.

Climbing the back stairs, Mr. Zwerling passed his landing and went up to the top. The door was unlocked. Max left the loft neat and there was a moment of her perfume in the air. He liked that but there was stuffiness too. He poled the skylight open. Max had gone up to Provincetown in June when one of her artist friends promised her a job. Mr. Zwerling did not know what the job was but Max had written twice. She would be back by September. Sweltering in New York, he and Emmett accepted this as more than reasonable. (Mr. Zwerling studied advertisements for the Catskill resorts every June, pursuing Emmett around the store with them. Emmett refused to go and Mr. Zwerling would not leave him.)

There were tools spread out on newspaper by the water closet. Emmett was changing Max's toilet. It had become cracked and stained over time. He was patching and painting the ceiling too as another surprise for her. Mr. Zwerling's excuse in coming up was to oil Max's typewriter. It was an Underwood that had sat downstairs behind the Sherwin-Willams sign. (Cover The Earth, the sign said.) Mr. Zwerling intended to work on the Underwood but until Max said she wanted to learn to typewrite he'd never got around to it. He enjoyed this repair more than many others.

"Could be I missed my calling."

Max had bought a typing manual at the library sale. (She had a shorthand instruction book too. Mr. Zwerling could not picture her in an office taking dictation.) The platen on the Underwood was badly pitted and the space bar was broken off but Max proudly demonstrated her first attempts at touch typing.

Mr. Zwerling wrote to Underwood about new parts but was asked to be patient. The company had switched to making rifles during the war and had not recovered inventory for older models. The Underwood vice-president who wrote back had a very distinctive signature.

"Handwriting like that is worth saving," Mr. Zwerling said. (Emmett frowned: was there anything this man would not keep?)

The letter and envelope went in Mr. Zwerling's correspondence file. (He was pleased to create a new folder and wrote Underwood, in all capitals, on the flap with his carpenter's pencil.)

A train was coming. The trains moved slowly as a rule and the rumbling created was sustained. If they disturbed Max she had never said so. For those who had grown up with the train it was something in the background, more than a racket but less than a landslide. When the train passed he heard a tugboat. He'd forgotten that the *Brittannic* was in port. It was a good reason to check the hatchway.

On the roof he found the usual tracings of soot left by the train. The breeze swirled a few particles onto his shirt. The flags of the *Brittannic* were at full mast. He was in time for the sailing and he watched as sacks of mail were hauled on board from the post office boat. Mr. Zwerling supposed the ship would be in England in a week.

He remembered there might have been a girl in their family. Her name was Minna and she was a distant cousin who had written to Mr. Zwerling's father. She came third class on the *Luisitania*, the voyage previous to the fatal one. Minna never made it out of quarantine, dying in a ward on Ellis Island of something unspecified.

His father said the *Luisitania* was a beautiful ocean liner. He knew one of the stewards who came from ironmongers at home. This man liked to visit the hardware store when the *Luisitania* was tied up at the pier. (A busman's holiday, Mr. Zwerling thought, we're all like that.) Spick and span sort, the elder Mr. Zwerling said of the steward, not a hair out of place. The steward was not seen again after the *Luisitania* left for its last voyage. Mr. Zwerling's father assumed he went down with his ship.

Mr. Zwerling was glad he'd come up. It was cooler on the roof and he was at leisure to wait for the *Brittannic* to depart. There were hours when no price could be put upon silence or even upon living. September would come soon enough and Max would be back with them. He did not believe he might ever really ask her. It was enough to think that he might. And though it was many years since anyone had mentioned his mouth, those instances were enough to last a lifetime. The tugboats were assembling. It was a sight worth seeing. His father had many good ideas and closing the store on shabbos was one.

1972

When Marianne Moore died in early February the library on Leroy Street held a small gathering to remember her. Miss Moore had worked at the Leroy Street branch in the 1920's when she was living with her mother on adjacent St. Luke's Place. Miss Eve Svenson was a young girl then, residing with her parents around the corner on Morton Street. She was a bookish child and was often in the library for one reason or another. Eve remembered Miss Moore very well as kind and ladylike. Not really the Village type, she never neglected to say, but then, of course, who truly is? That is a profound question.

Miss Moore had been radical in her poems and methodology and her championing of the modern but she was equally at home where tea was served with buttercream cake. That was Eve Svenson's opinion and she found it generous and pertinent. (She took pride in being at all costs to the point.)

Miss Svenson graduated from Hunter College with a teaching degree. By that time Miss Moore and her mother had moved to Brooklyn. Gradually, Miss Moore became famous in her own particular manner. Eve Svenson took a proprietary inter-est in this career. She had newspaper articles and several first editions. She still lived in her old apartment though it was no longer a cold water flat but an altogether commodious one bed-room with central heating and a glimpse of the elbow where Morton, in the delightful Village way, bends gently towards Bedford Street.

She was three years from retirement and though tired of teaching and of children, her plan was to stick it out. Her pen-sion, she hoped, would allow her to travel though in recent years the furthest she went was the Gotham Book Mart where the neighborhood she found was increasingly commercial and Hebraic. The library on Leroy Street was a Saturday pleasure but one where she sometimes pressed the Marianne Moore connection of old too strongly.

"Oh brother, here she comes."

If Miss Svenson was spoken of dismissively she did not notice. She knew her advice was helpful and well received. And really, there was no one who could make a backward ragamuffin understand the Dewey decimal system so well as she.

January had been very cold. Max did not like to ask Mr. Zwerling to keep the heat on at night. He was frugal in that respect and he and Emmett did not seem to notice the cold when they were inside. Some nights she kept the oven running but not too high because Mr. Zwerling paid the bill.

Mother and daughter had both been sick all month. Max had bought Salome a goose down sleeping bag for Christmas. It was a sale item from Weiss and Mahoney, there was something wrong with the zipper closure, and Salome's bed went beside the oven with the sleeping bag on the mattress. When she was in school, in the springtime, Salome heard about sleepaway summer camps. She told her mother but Max never managed to put the money aside. (They set out once for Freedomland in the Bronx; there were musical advertisements on the radio for the amusement park. They got lost. Max had trouble with the subway if she had to change lines.)

The cough and sore throat they shared would not go away. Max had headaches and felt too weak to look for work.

There was still money from her Christmas jobs. The first was at a waterbed store on MacDougal Alley. (Pollock lived across the mews when Tony first introduced them. You're a cutie, Pollock said.) The manager did not take her social security number and she worked on commission. He did not give her good shifts, they were mostly in the morning. A young woman named Tracy came in about noon or later every day. She wore high boots and a short skirt and no underwear. If a man was looking at a waterbed she sat on it, spreading her knees apart.

"After one night," she explained, "you'll never want anything else."

That's salesmanship, the manager said. He told Max she had no moxie. Whenever she did sell a bed he argued about her percentage. There was also the Bowl & Board on Christopher Street. She liked it there though it was minimum wage. There were textiles and wooden utensils from other countries, from India and Japan. (Azuma was like this too.) She was given a black apron that said Bowl & Board and there was a Christmas party with wine and Italian hero sandwiches for the employees. During the Christmas rush she got extra hours and she worked until New Year's because of returns. She hoped they would keep her on but they could not.

As she grew older, Max was more aware of not having completed high school. Department stores once did not ask but now had personnel offices that did. They said they were sorry but she could not be considered without a diploma. Max was turned away by the maritime union and St. Vincent's hospital. Twice she had tried night school but each time failed the equivalency exam. The exams made her anxious as if she were being hunted.

She did have trouble with numbers. At the Bowl & Board they took her off the cash register because of her difficulty with addition. Max wondered at anyone who could multiply or divide in their head. It seemed like a magic trick to her.

Mr. Zwerling filled in her tax form in the years when she had work on the books. Any refund she received seemed altogether wonderful and she and Salome painted the town. They went out for grilled cheese sandwiches and ice cream sodas. (At a Chinese restaurant Salome was enthralled with chopsticks though she could not manipulate them. She saved her fortune cookie and kept it under her pillow until it broke. Her fortune said silence is a good friend who never betrays.)

Max had a long association with a stationary store on Seventh Avenue. They contracted with home typists to do resumes and dissertations. She was paid by the page. Max was never very fast but she was very accurate. She enjoyed an assignment with a beginning and an end. It was her preference to work alone.

There were years when she delivered telephone books but the man she worked for had passed away suddenly and his business had closed. Before he died he gave Max an electric typewriter. It was an Olivetti he had bought for her. It increased her speed and Salome loved the sound of it as Max typed standing up at the restaurant rack. (She took Marlboro breaks away from the machine. A manuscript had been sent back because it smelled of cigarette smoke.) The Olivetti was a modern design and nearly the same shade of yellow as patches of the large de Kooning wall.

Her editor at the New York *Post* retired and they no longer took her notices. There was a shift in what interested readers. She tried to write about other music but could not place anything. (She wrote about Tim Buckley who was working with a jazz guitarist and vibraphonist but could not catch the mood. She did like his voice.)

It was bebop that Max loved, though it was difficult to explain how that came to pass. Those hotels she lived in earlier had thin walls. She heard Symphony Sid on the radio in another room introducing "Out of Nowhere." That was the first time she held her breath listening. It often happened afterward. When she heard Bud Powell she thought the floor was moving beneath her and he remained her dearest jazz companion. At the loft she dropped one of his 78's. It broke but she kept the center label as a paperweight. Bud Powell died a few days after Frank O'Hara in 1966. All that week Max felt her world had partly come to an end.

Max did not care for Slug's Saloon. It was on East Third Street and she was not at ease on those streets at night. But McCoy Tyner was playing and she wanted to go. She had not been to a club for many months. The weather was still cold but both she and Salome were feeling better. Her head did not ache but her nose was still red. Max did not wear her black wrap dress. It no longer fit and Slug's was not that kind of place. And she did not meet men any longer. It was a long walk from Tenth Avenue. Max was not known there. She paid for the cover, which came with two drinks, and stood at the bar.

"You look frozen," the bartender said.

On his own he made her a hot whiskey with lemon. The drink ran through her and seemed to relieve all the ache inside. Slug's was grimy and she hoped not to use the toilet. A musician had been killed there the week before. He was a trumpeter, shot to death by his girlfriend. Across the bar there was a man she assumed to be plain clothes. Slugs was said to be a good place to score.

McCoy Tyner opened with "My Funny Valentine." His technique had grown softer, Max thought, since the harder bop she recalled. She supposed he was getting older too though he was yet strong and good looking. Max had her second whiskey and listened with her eyes closed, her shoulders moving slightly. This was what she had missed. It would go on forever if she had her way. The bartender gave her another whiskey, knocking gently on the bar with his knuckles. She felt as if the keyboard were inside her.

The pianist took a break. Max had not removed her coat and her face was very warm. She was tired from the walk and the drinks had been too strong. She lurched away from the bar and went outside. The cold night air struck her and she was dizzy. She went right instead of left, walking weakly towards Avenue C. At the corner she didn't know where she was. It was unfamiliar and the street light was broken. When she turned, a man came from between two cars and shoved her against a brick wall. He banged her head. He wanted her purse.

"Don't hurt me," she said. "Please don't hurt me."

Max had no purse. She had three dollars. She held it out in her hand. The man took it and was angry. He stomped on her leg. She fell and he kicked her in the stomach. Max rolled over as he ran away. She wet herself.

Miss Eve Swenson had a tiresome week. What she called her commute to work had become an ordeal. Her school, P. S. 41, was on West Eleventh Street. She walked, first to Bleecker and then to Cornelia and then up Sixth Avenue. She was proud of her steadfastness. (Like the couriers of the General Post Office facade, Miss Svenson had her appointed rounds. The quotation is from Herodotus, as she liked to indicate.) In fine weather the walk was once invigorating.

These days, however, the weather and the streets were not what they had been. The hippies and dirt had taken over the sidewalks and winter seemed never to end. Miss Svenson expected to be accosted and her expectation was often met. There was an all night delicatessen next to St. Joseph's Church. People of all sorts slept on the steps of the church, picnicking from the deli. They were intoxicated at all hours. She was asked for money. On at least one occasion Miss Swenson was asked to dance. She did not expect much from the Catholics but they could, she thought, sweep these creatures from their own doorstep. The recent cold had made the loungers more desperate. One of them demanded a dollar and when she refused he called her a name she had never been called. He modified it with old. She looked for a policeman but of course there was not one to be found.

At school, in the teacher's lounge, she complained to anyone who would listen. This was not many. The previous fall there was a riot at Attica, the penitentiary upstate. Prisoners had rebelled and threatened to kill the hostages they had taken. After dithering for several days the Governor found his manhood (as Miss Svenson put it) and sent in the state police. Many of the rioting prisoners were shot down. Miss Svenson felt they all should have been killed. She was forthright about this in the teacher's lounge. As many of her colleagues at school were of the same persuasion as the prisoners she felt they did not agree. That was their privilege of course but it was no reason to ostracize her. She did not like to think of herself as shunned but it did appear that way. Miss Swenson wished to see the longhaired bums on the steps of St. Joseph's taken care of too.

Miss Svenson had her hair done Saturday morning for the Marianne Moore commemoration. She had expected the library to call but they had not. This she attributed to the director whom Eve considered to be in over her head on Leroy Street and careless. She arrived at noon with her two first editions (*Collected Poems* from 1951 and the later *Like a Bulwark*) and the two signed letters she had received from Miss Moore. A large bulletin board was given over to photographs and newspaper stories and to dust covers from Miss Moore's books. (One of the latter was another *Like a Bulwark* that Eve deemed sun faded, unlike her own.)

There was a table with apple cider and thumbprint cookies and an urn of coffee. Recordings were played: Miss Moore interviewed on WYNC and Miss Moore reciting her poem about the Brooklyn Dodgers. A young girl (about twelve and possibly a stutterer, Miss Svenson concluded, she won't make a career of this) read one of Miss Moore's translations of the fables of Fontaine. Eve positioned herself by the card catalog, determined to display her goods. She tried to catch the eye of a reporter from *The Villager*, recognizing him from an event at P. S. 41. He passed her twice and finally she pulled at his coat sleeve. He nodded politely, looked at her signed letters, and walked away. He hadn't even brought a camera, an omission she could not understand. There were a great many noisy children and when Eve decided on a thumbprint cookie they had all been eaten.

Max worried that Salome did not speak a lot. Even on a cold day indoors she might not hear her daughter's voice for hours. She sometimes forgot she was there. Max was not vocal either and in the days after the robbery on East Third Street she was especially quiet. She was bruised and her kidneys hurt and they had used up their aspirin. The drugstore was on Eighth Avenue but she wouldn't send Salome when she was beginning to feel better.

On Saturday morning Max was less sore. Salome hoped they could take a walk. They had missed Valentine's Day at the library, which Salome enjoyed. There were Valentine hearts and other cutouts and Valentine cookies for everyone. Salome was too old for the children's party but she liked to watch the others.

It was good to be outside. We're fancy free, Max said. She and her daughter walked slowly, holding hands. It was surprising to find the library so busy but when Max saw the pictures of Marianne Moore she understood. She was grateful for the coffee. Because it was a diuretic she'd stopped drinking it. Salome had cider and a thumbprint cookie and they listened to a young girl reciting one of Miss Moore's poems. (The girl was nervous but carried on to the end. She was never applauded before. She blushed and Salome and her mother clapped harder.) Max was happy that someone like Marianne Moore was being celebrated.

Miss Svenson disliked seeing the library used by vagrants. They came in to stay warm, she knew, and took up space at the tables. She was prepared to leave, not having removed her coat. Marianne Moore's day, she felt, had gone very wrong. The library director was unkind. She, Eve, was the only person present who had actually known Miss Moore and she, Eve, was not invited to participate in any meaningful way. It should also have been a private affair without all these people from the street.

It was time for her to depart but as Miss Svenson turned, Salome bumped into her. Cider from the paper cup spilled on Miss Svenson's coat sleeve and onto one of the first editions. Max came forward with her handkerchief and wiped at the sleeve.

"I'm sorry," she said. "It's not too wet I think."

Miss Svenson looked at her. "Is she with you?"

"Yes, she's my daughter. Salome is her…"

"Your daughter? She's not very clean. You do see that, don't you?"

Max turned her head. "I'm sorry, I didn't..."

"I can smell her. I can smell her across the room. What do you think this building is? This is a library. It is a sanctuary, a place of learning. It is not a home for derelicts. It's people like you who have destroyed..."

Miss Svenson knew she had made herself clear. She had spoken forcefully but without raising her voice. She held her books and letters and left, no longer so displeased with her morning. Salome had taken her paper cup to the trash bin. She went back to her mother. Some of the children were assembled for a singalong. When that was over, Max and Salome left to go home. They never went to the library on Leroy Street again.

1952

S ummer was coming on. Max met Margaret at Franklin Simon after work and they walked down to Union Square together. Max bought a lipstick while she was waiting for Margaret and they both tried it out. Margaret carried a compact. They were thinking about the Armenian place next to Ohrbach's but weren't very hungry.

It was not so warm yet but warm enough to remind you how warm it would get in a week or two and there goes your appetite pronto. Instead they talked over going to Provincetown again. Margaret, for her part, could not decide. On the one hand the store cut her hours for July and August, so she might as well take the furlough. On the other hand leaving her boyfriend off the leash for two months might well result in him acquiring another social disease. He had a knack for this. As for Max it had more to do with Tony who had been released from Pilgrim State and was on the loose.

"What is that he's doing?"

It was macrame. Margaret did not care for painters and it did not matter how often Max told her Tony was not a painter.

"Same difference. They're all jerks anyway."

Max had run into Tony at the Cedar. He was trying to inter-est the bartender in plant hangers. As the bar did not have plants, Tony met with resistance to his new venture. He was also mak-ing placemats and coasters. It was all lumpy for the most part. Tony was not unpopular so no one asked how the loony bin was. He had trouble completely remembering Max. She was there but it was muddled in his mind. (Max did not know the nature of the medication he was given.) He did grasp, however, that she was somehow friendly.

"Right, how are you? We had fun, huh? Wait right here."

She didn't. She left the Cedar and went home. It was noisy anyway and she only went because the drinks were cheap and she knew people. The next week she saw Tony outside Brentano's. He grabbed her and asked why she was mad at him.

"It's driving me nuts," he said.

Perhaps not the best choice of words. But that didn't mat-ter, he had news, he was going to Provincetown. He'd seen Hans and Hans had an opening because someone had been drafted. (There was another war but unlike the other one nobody paid attention to it.) Hans would have him clean up and take over a drawing class for the beginners. Tony was a good draftsman and though not everyone would say so, Hans did.

Max got caught up with Tony again the way people got caught up with him when he was thriving. "I was there last year. I went with my friend Margaret."

Tony's eyes glittered. "Did you drive? Have you got a car?"

Max felt stuck. Margaret would not like this. Tony sensed a shift in her demeanor. "I remembered about us," he said. "We went to the Cloisters and they yelled at me for pulling up that mandrake or something. Right, huh? That's us."

It was more than yelling. Tony had nearly hit the guard and they got away only by luck. But he remembered that she had been with him.

"I don't know if we'll go this year," Max said. "Maybe..."

Margaret's boyfriend worked for *Fortune*, which she said was like a goldfish bowl for girls that lived at the Barbizon and had big brown eyes. The editors and writers stood around the bowl watching them wiggle and when they saw one they liked they picked it out and swallowed it. Margaret caught her boyfriend with one of these goldfish coming out of Brownie's (this goldfish was a health and physical culture kook of all things with the bazooms to prove it) so she told Max P-Town was okay with her.

Margaret was steamed like King Crab with a side of slaw. She went out to Astoria to get her Ford sedan from her father. Mr. Stephanos kept it in trim for her in gratitude for her staying in Manhattan and not in Queens where she would boss him around. He put two demijohns of ouzo from his restaurant in the trunk too.

Max left a note for Tony with the day bartender at the Cedar to the effect that they would leave from outside the high school on Irving Place Tuesday morning. (Margaret lived around the corner.) Max was instructed by Margaret to say in the note that they would get going at nine sharp and nine sharp meant nine sharp and bring gas money. Max used different phrasing as she assumed Tony would be late and would have no gas money.

At a quarter-past nine Margaret was antsy. At nine-thirty she was hopeful. At nine forty-five she had looked through the Spiegel catalog twice and was ready to leave.

"Shall we?"

At that moment a cab pulled up. Tony got out on one side with a fishing rod. A second man emerged from the other side with a duffel bag and a dripping milk crate.

"Guy from the army," Tony said. "He can sleep it off in the back."

This was not encouraging. Margaret was about to say something when the cab driver hopped out like a flamenco dancer. By this time both men were expertly in Margaret's Ford and the cab driver stared at her and at Max and then at both of them simultaneously, one eye on each. (The cab driver had that expectant look like a head waiter or a girl standing at the altar.) Max paid him. It seemed to be the most convenient thing to do.

Because Margaret was still par-boiled at her boyfriend it did not take much to get her bubbling again. Later though, when they were on Route 1 and passing church steeples and picket fences and the cooler summer look of everything, she felt better. She never tired of that road and the people and things on it. Tony fell asleep up front. He was no rose and he snored. The second man was stretched in the back, quietly at rest. When Max looked over her shoulder the man's face with only a slight stubble was that of a child. They stopped in Connecticut for gas and a Coke and to use the toilet. The men remained asleep. Margaret and Max leaned against the Ford with straws in their bottles. The screen door of the general store clicked gently.

"Ten years since I left Indiana," Max said.

A farmer was selling melons from the back of a truck. The young girl with him seemed to be his daughter, her hair tied up in a bright green bandana with a twist poking out the back. The bandana looked to have been ironed that morning.

"Look how pretty she is, Margaret. Don't you think so? Don't you think she's the prettiest thing?"

Margaret finished her Coke with a menacing sound. "Don't get that way. Whatever you do, don't get that way."

They did not stop again until the Cape Cod Canal. Margaret was aces at naming all the state capitals and listing Bette Davis movies. She told jokes and only mentioned her boyfriend in reference to his funeral. (She explained the process of drawing and quartering. Not nice at all.) At the canal the men came around. Everyone got out to stretch and Tony went behind a tree. His friend did as well but went further away. He was chipper. Tony was a wreck.

"Where are we?"

The friend came back from his tree and asked if they would like a bite. As they were on the tow path beneath the bridge this seemed a hollow invitation at first but the friend brought the milk crate from the car. It was still dripping.

"Jack knows a cook at Delmonico's," Tony said. "We stopped there last night when the kitchen was closing."

In his duffel bag Jack had silverware and water glasses wrapped in a tablecloth. The ice in the milk crate had melted but the food was cool. There was beer and a bottle of Veuve Clicquot, steak sandwiches and lobster rolls and deviled eggs.

The knives and forks had the Delmonico crest as did the salt and pepper shakers.

The tablecloth was spread out and the men each had a beer, too hungover to do more than pick. Margaret did not like to see food wasted and Max loved both steak and lobster in no particular order. Jack opened the champagne and the time passed as they lay on their sides below the traffic on the Sagamore Bridge. It was cooler than New York and that and the food and wine put Margaret in a good mood.

"Can't you just picture that bum eating chickenless chow mein and meatless goulash just because this particular goldfish is a C-cup? What a chump. She can have him."

She was in such a good mood she told Max about a dish of frog legs Provencale at Le Poissonnier when she was seventeen. The frog lost its legs and she lost her virginity and she'd been a sucker for clarified butter ever since.

After a cigarette she and Max dozed, leaning against each other for an hour and the breeze raised goosebumps on their bare arms.

They had a room on Cromwell Lane around the back of the Barnstable House. They'd had it before. The room had two iron beds and oil lamps and was good enough for sleeping. Margaret had left a Steinbeck novel under the mattress the previous year and when they were unpacked she began reading where she left off.

The arrangement was they used the hall bathrooms in the hotel as long as they were quick. For some reason the Barnstable

House bar was called Tubby's. It was Portuguese and cheap and there was excellent bread and caldo verde for any meal. Tony left his fishing pole in the Ford and went in search of Hans. They did not know what to do with Jack but he solved this by saying thank you and leaving with his duffel bag.

"I believe that man is shy," Margaret said.

She left it at that. She was satisfied because Jack had paid his way with lunch, leaving the Delmonico's silverware and the salt and pepper shakers. As for Tony she hoped not to see him again for the rest of the summer but that was not how it turned out.

Hans gave Tony a class right away. Tony needed a place to work but Hans nixed using the school at night as there was no way of telling what it would look like in the morning. That was Tony's reputation even among those who were tolerant of his behavior.

Now Hans, among other things, was frisky with the girls. He hadn't succeeded with Margaret in previous years but it was not for lack of trying. He wasn't sure why he did. On the plus side Margaret was leggy, that's good, but on the minus she was mouthy, which is not good if you are a man who does not like backtalk. Margaret specialized in backtalk and didn't like painters anyway. In addition she was off men for the duration.

"I'll be on the beach all day and in bed by nine," she confided. "And if I'm not tortoiseshell by September kiddo it won't be my fault."

The Barnstable House was owned by the Maciel brothers who were well known along the Outer Cape for the quality of their unpleasantness. They referred to themselves as old world Portuguese, which did not say much for the old world. They mistrusted most people and disliked the summer because they had to hire more people they did not trust.

Germano was Cape Verdean and completely trustworthy, though that too made the brothers suspicious. Germano had eyes the color of olives and he was happy to see Max again. They'd been simpatico the year before. Unfortunately, by the time Max arrived Germano, a very fine cook, had plans of earning his way back to Cape Verde on a freighter. He lived with Como who sold whale knuckles and postcards and liked to be known as a picturesque old salt as opposed to a falling down old rummy. (Como's breath was wicked. It would, some said, set the windmill going in an old Dutch painting.)

The night before he left Germano and Max sat on the dunes with a bottle of rum. They had drunk from the same bottle other times. Rum is warm and sticky that way. Germano talked about home, something Max never did. She liked to hear about origins but had nothing to contribute. Germano said he was sorry he had not made a go of it in Provincetown where no one bothered you but Max did not think this was true. She knew a drifter when she heard one. When Max awoke in the morning, chilled and gritty on the sand, Germano was gone.

It took a few weeks before Tony ran into trouble. (After Germano decamped, Tony moved in with Como, not a prescription for calm and sobriety. Some nights the whale knuckles really flew. At this point Tony had probably ceased taking the librium.)

Gregory, who referred to himself as *une petite tapette*, ran a plein air class near the town wharf. He knew little about painting but his students were women who did not notice. He looked the part in a smock and floppy Manet hat and never said anything too critical as his students paid dutifully by the day.

Hans said he was a joke, which was perhaps putting it too strongly. Gregory was not poaching on anyone and plein air (as has undoubtedly been said sometime or other) is like the Nutcracker: no one can work up the energy to dislike it.

Gregory was in Tubby's every night spending the money he'd made that day. He treated his friends and his friends treated everyone else. One evening he and Tony got into a tiff about something. It didn't take a lot as Gregory was not Tony's idea of masculine. The argument sputtered out but there was some giggling from Gregory's crowd and Tony could not bear to be laughed at. The next day Tony broke up Gregory's class by riding a bicycle through it.

Box easels were flying everywhere and one woman who was absorbed in a cumulus cloud may have suffered a sprain. Tony was arrested but it was for stealing the bicycle. Gregory was connected to somebody, a selectman it might have been, but did not complain. (As a smallish man with a slight lisp he had learned early that complaining would do no good.) He supposedly told his class this goes on in France all the time and they should be inspired. But Tony was in the pokey and bail was seventy-five dollars. He might as well have run into a speed trap.

Max went to see Tony. He was miserable with a first class katzenjammer but not especially repentant. He confessed to siphoning off a milk bottle's worth of ouzo from the demijohn whereupon he stayed up all night on the beach drinking. (As opposed to going home and sharing with Como.) That's why breaking up the plein air class seemed like a good idea in the morning. Now it didn't. Tony was afraid of losing his connection with Hans. The latter was from Austria and serious, grave even, where art was concerned. In other words he was long on lectures and short on American high-jinks.

"Go find Jack," Tony said.

Max did not mention the missing ouzo to Margaret who was already grumpy because someone had stolen the curb feelers from her Ford. (The Ford had whitewalls and she was careful about them.) As for Jack, Max had seen him once in passing since the day they arrived. He was scraping and painting the cast iron fence in front of the Star of the Sea in payment for sleeping in the church basement. It seems Jack spoke adequate French so he communicated easily enough with the Portuguese fisherman who apparently found him a man after their own independent seafaring hearts.

Father Silva told Max that Jack had moved (after finishing the fence) to an oyster shack on the bay. Father Silva asked her to wait a moment and came back with sandwiches and a bottle of wine. The oyster shack was about a half-mile up the shore and Jack was sitting on an upside down bucket reading *Swann's Way*. You could say the oyster shack smelled like the sea; you could also say it smelled like fish.

There were shell mounds and herring gulls poking in them for bits of meat. The gulls didn't seem to mind Jack. The sandwiches were chorizo and onion and very tasty. Max and Jack passed the wine back and forth. As she was sitting with him she had a great desire to paint her toenails, something she did not normally do. (This may have been the writing on the wall.)

She told Jack what had happened to Tony, which did not appear to either surprise or distress him. But like everyone else he did not have seventy-five dollars. He told Max he would come see her later. He'd have a swim and try to think of something. Max went back to her room that now seemed opulent compared to the oyster shack. Margaret was there. She'd been to the police to complain about her curb feelers. They cost very little but they were her curb feelers and as a woman she didn't like the idea of a stranger using them. Max told her what happened to Tony and about her visit to Jack.

"This should be rich," Margaret said.

Hans was not happy. He saw Max on the Barnstable House porch and asked why Tony was in jail. For lack of anything else Max said he was doing research. Hans had a way of looking unhappy that was all his own. He was preparing to be more disgruntled when Jack came down the street with two little men who were holding a wooden sign. Jack commissioned a Portuguese sign-maker, payment to be arranged later, to announce a party at the hotel. The sign was striking. There was a border of azulejos in a starfish pattern. It was blue and gold at the edges, a cloudy gray at the center, blending Portuguese tilework with New England clapboard. Hans ceased being Hans for a blessed moment and studied the sign.

"Magnificent," he said.

Max and Jack went to the wharf and propped the sign up. Jack left but was back shortly with a school bell and business cards from the Seamen's Bank and an unlicensed dentist. They rang the bell and sold tickets for a dollar. They wrote ADMIT ONE on the backs of the business cards and sometimes ADMIT TWO. The sign said there would be a raffle and Max asked what the prize was.

"The sign," Jack said.

Max discovered that one got used to Jack very quickly. He'd hunted up the local loan shark who had an interest in getting Tony out of jail as Tony already owed him money. The loan shark was married to a former actress from the Provincetown Playhouse days who went native and never returned to New York. She volunteered to do a reading at Tubby's to help out.

"That's exactly what we need," Jack told her, "beauty and style in one expressive package. You'll be divine, like Duse, like...."

The loan shark and his wife were so pleased they bought four tickets as well as ponying up the bail money in advance. Max and Jack went to the magistrate and paid the bail (the magistrate bought two tickets) and Tony was released. They explained about the raffle and so forth and Tony said he could use a party to cheer him up because it was sad to be imprisoned on bread and water. (The jail food was the best Tony ate all summer.)

Jack mentioned that there was no point in throwing a get-out-of-jail party if that person was already out of jail and attending the party. Tony did not see it that way, he wanted to come. Jack suggested he could show up at the end and maybe make a speech but Tony wasn't having that. (Tony had no difficulty shooting his mouth off but a speech was another matter.) He was angry and walked off. He seemed to think if he hadn't gone to the trouble of being arrested his friends would not be having all this fun. It was tempting to say "that's painters for you" but Tony wasn't a painter.

One of the Maciel brothers had a wife who did most of the work at the hotel. They kept busy spying on their workers and their guests, somewhat like house detectives. In fairness, long years of dealing with artists had left them more inclined to skepticism than they might have been on their own. (Possibly, but maybe not.) The hotel bar and the lobby and all the rooms had one thing in common. There were paintings on the walls and these paintings were all from artists who could not pay their bill. The stories were all the same.

The artists promised to buy them back the next summer but either the artists did not stay there again or had changed their style and did not want the paintings or most often still did not have the money. All of the Maciel paintings were for sale but most of the hotel's guests were artists or writers who are traditionally the hardest sell of all. Once in a while the Maciels tried to pay a food or liquor bill with a painting but never had any luck. So this did not make them look warmly on the art world. Max was afraid the brothers would not be happy with their plan for the party.

"Well then," Jack said, "we won't tell them."

So they did not or at least not directly. On the way back to Tubby's they stopped to see Gregory, whose many friends liked a lively time. Jack wanted to be sure of their attendance. Gregory was only a little sore about his class being broken up; he was mostly hurt that Tony did that to him. (The army rejected Gregory three times during the war, deeming him unfit. He was greatly dejected and compensated by giving blood every week.)

Jack worked on Gregory and it was something to watch. Jack looked like a beachcomber but a beachcomber perhaps out of Raphael or Botticelli. His trousers needed a belt and his rope sandals were floppy but once Jack's arm crept around Gregory's shoulder the petite tapette was won over.

Jack had spent time in Paris after the war and this was all Gregory needed to hear. Max understood, if not fully, that you don't often get to see the dots connected in action. (As Margaret would say he could really sling the bull.) After Gregory was taken care of, they needed an inconspicuous receptacle for donations, something the Maciel brothers might not notice. Jack began to whistle, it sounded like the "Golliwog's Cakewalk." Jack said he had an idea.

"See you at six o'clock."

Max wanted to wash her hair. She sat on the back porch of the hotel waiting for the hall shower to be free. She began to think of the next letter she would write to Mr. Zwerling, which he would read out loud to Emmett. There were days when she missed Tenth Avenue, when she missed the pulsing of the viaduct and the hooting of the tugboats in the harbor. All winter she had worked at the Homestead in the kitchen. Only men worked in the dining room. She was never adept at prep work (mostly she washed dishes) and the cooks joshed her but a family owned the restaurant and they liked to have people they liked. She felt lucky but did not know if she would go back there again.

It was Margaret in the shower room. She was tall and she was a good looking girl, wet or dry. Margaret was tired of hearing about Tony (whom she thought should have been left another day or two in the cooler) so Max talked about Jack instead. Margaret worked a towel around her head and said she would throw in a fiver at the party. For her money you could not beat Gregory and his nancy boys for a good time.

"But keep this in mind before you go off the deep end honey. This Jack of yours is a buttered baked potato if ever I've seen one and, believe me, I've seen them. We're born with two curses and the second one is men. You can't do anything about the first one but try to stay clear of the other as much as possible."

There were more comings and goings in town when the Boston steamer arrived. So when Tubby's began to fill up around six-thirty it did not seem unusual. Only one Maciel was there, helping behind the bar. First Hans came with some of his crowd and the Maciel brother was afflicted with the tic the sight of painters gave him. But as long as people were paying for their drinks he was satisfied. The party sign was set on an easel and two teen-age boys came in carrying spotlights. These were set up around the pool table.

Gregory came in with his bunch and then Father Silva and his church ladies who brought baskets of food. Tables were pushed together and wine bottles with candles appeared. The loan shark and his wife were next. She carried a Samuel French playbook and asked Max where her dressing room was. The Maciel brothers had been assured (presumably by Jack) that it was the anniversary of Father Silva's ordination. That was difficult to be a killjoy about.

Three musicians proceeded to set up along with a vampy woman named Theda who promised fado in several languages. Some tourists inquired if it was a private party and were told it was anything but that. The tourists stayed. It was quickly stuffy in the bar and Max went out on the front porch. She saw Jack coming and immediately felt a way she should not feel. Sometimes they are a block away and you feel your heart take a dive. That's how she felt. She supposed it was too late. Jack was smoking a cigar and walking a St. Bernard. The St. Bernard had a small barrel around his neck with a slot in it. Jack said the dog's name was Buster.

"Hi Buster, where did you come from?"

"The Alps," Jack said.

Jack borrowed a trumpet from the musicians and blew an adequate high C. That got the room's attention and he announced that Buster needed an operation. He pointed to the dog and looked mournful and Buster looked mournful too. Someone asked what kind of operation and Jack said Buster was a female and so that was an indelicate question. (As Max had just seen Buster lift his leg on the bar rail she had her doubts about this.)

It was obvious that Jack had enjoyed a few and was not for the moment concerned with details. He explained that donations could be left in the barrel but only folding money please as coins might give Buster a stiff neck.

He introduced the actress and set her up at the pool table with the spots on her. She did a scene from *Anna Christie* to enthusiastic applause as many in the audience owed her husband money. Margaret, who did not owe her husband money, said it was O'Neill in a hot room and all right if you like that sort of thing. The actress was ready with an encore but Jack brought on the fado singer who moaned "Mouraria" until even the Maciel brother was sniffling.

The raffle was never mentioned and the sign disappeared. At the end, when only a few guests remained, Jack played the piano. Max loved a keyboard and hands that can fly over them. After the bar closed she went back to the oyster shack with Jack and the dog. They'd forgotten about Tony.

As the summer went on Max heard little about Tony. She wondered if that was ominous as this sometimes preceded a storm. A quiet, retiring Tony was not what anyone expected. Hans said he was much improved and close to conscientious. What Hans paid him provided two squares per day (little more than beans and brown bread, both of which came out of a can) and he'd moved into a garage because Como had offended his honor somehow. It was up an alley behind Bradford Street. What Tony was paying for the garage was anyone's guess. On a sunny day, if the barn doors were open, he had seven or eight hours of good working light.

"More than enough," he said. "Like Michaelangelo, I'm not a painter."

Max had never been read to in her life and Jack liked reading out loud. He also could recite a great deal from memory and knew the verses and additional lyrics to hundreds of songs. Aside from that he was not conversational and Max did not feel encouraged to ask anything too personal. As for Margaret, taking a longish outlook, she appreciated men who were not yappy but overall did not feel it was a good thing.

"With some of these guys," she said, "the suitcase comes out one day. And then one day the suitcase is full. And the next day he's gone. And then there's some other guys, you know, you never even see the suitcase."

Jack had his single piece of luggage and there was very little in it. (He also kept a Gladstone bag with the head of housekeeping at the Hotel Pennsylvania. It held Charvet shirts and ties. That was for train trips and Europe.) Max did not want to think about the duffel bag though the sight of some things brought it to mind.

She stopped to see Tony at the garage. She thought she should because she was happy, a little nervous, but happy overall. Tony never really was, happy that is. By way of hospitality Tony opened a can of Boston brown bread at both ends and plopped it onto a plate. It looked somewhat like Jack's duffel bag. Max said she'd eaten. The garage was rough and it was in the middle of a junkyard. Max scratched her leg on the leads of a car battery. Tony was serene (preceding the up and at'em phase that led to the decline) and in a mood to talk.

"Studebaker," he said.

That was the name of the assemblage. The first thing Max noticed was Margaret's curb feelers. Tony admitted taking them the night he helped himself to the ouzo. He went through town whacking them on telephone poles and singing "Perfidia". (Later on, after Tony's death, after he had hanged himself with piano wire, "Studebaker" went to the Whitney. The curb feelers were a problem. Even well-adjusted adults, never mind children, could not resist twanging them. "Studebaker" had to have its own guard but some days, when the museum was quiet and that room empty, the guards too could not resist the temptation and gave the curb feelers a tweak.)

"It's going good, real good."

Max hoped that was true. When they were together on Weehawken Street you were listening to Brahams and suddenly the frequency changed to an advertisement for Burma Shave. Tony could not help it. There were times when he knew it was coming; there were times when he didn't. He touched Max's arm gently.

"I got sucker punched," he said, "real bad".

At the end of August there were mornings with a chill. Gregory's plein air students held their hats down with one hand as they worked. Margaret received a heartfelt note from her boyfriend, similar in sentiment and wording to the one he'd sent the year before. She was so moved she gave in to a sailor on leave from the submarine base in New London. (The sailor said all he wanted to do after his hitch was paint. Margaret said adios without regret.)

Hans closed up and the crowd at Tubby's waned. Jack made a reference to Key West. Max wondered if she made a mistake cleaning the oyster shack and washing the one window. Star of the Sea had their end-of-season rummage sale and she bought Jack a pair of trousers and a pullover. She'd kept his other things together with a needle and thread. He accepted this as he did everything else, politely, without emotion. Max was down to a few dollars from her summer grubstake and Margaret was ready to leave though she still had not finished *The Wayward Bus*. One night they polished off what was left of the ouzo.

"How about Friday? I can start at the store again Tuesday."

Max supposed so. She was the passenger, it was not her place to procrastinate. She tried to be casual and asked Jack if he'd like a ride back to New York. He said he'd take a raincheck. Something inside Max twinged, as there are men who collect rainchecks all their lives.

"I like to start fresh."

The morning they left Max felt queasy. She assumed it was in place of feeling something else. When they stopped for gas she went to the toilet and looked in the mirror. And then she vomited. She vomited a second time before they reached Manhattan. On Tenth Avenue she had several days of doubt. After a week she was sure and did not bother about the rabbit test. She also did not have the money.

"Sloppy Joe's, Duval Street; they'll know where to find me."

It was the last thing Jack said. Max thought about Key West through the cold months. She thought she would like it. She'd come to love salt water and people like Como who sold whale knuckles and postcards. She'd never learned to swim but her baby would. She would very nearly be a mermaid. Max wrote to Jack but did not say anything out of the way. She wanted to wait.

It was as well she did. When her child was born, six weeks premature, she saw that Jack was not the father. It was Germano.

"Silly me," she said.

Hans enjoyed lecturing on art subjects. One night at Tubby's he talked about Salome from the bible. Max remembered the story from Sunday school. She liked the name and called her daughter that. She worried about a hundred things. Many of them were the things she did not know how to do. The loft had one remaining blank wall; it would remain that way she thought. The nights, the long nights, when painters came and worked when the mood struck were over. It would never be like that again.

1969

Rain was predicted but Mr. Zwerling did not like the look of the sky. During the war he had taken his German-made barometer out under the viaduct and smashed it with his father's therapeutic claw hammer. Sweeping up the barometer pieces had been satisfying but for one reason or another he had never acquired another. Mr. Zwerling could repair a watch and set about several times building his own barometer (guided to some extent by a moldy issue of *Popular Mechanics* Emmett had been attempting to throw away for years) but other jobs intervened.

In one catalog he'd seen Black Forest weather houses with a peasant couple swinging out to indicate rain or shine. Mr. Zwerling sighed over those but they were just too *daytsh*. (As a lover of kitsch it was exasperating how much wonderfully insipid junk came from those *fakakta* Nazis.) He had thermometers (the store sold them) but there were days when nothing less than a good dependable barometer would do.

"Something's up. I can feel it."

As for Emmett, he assumed there would be precipitation and left it at that. He knew Mr. Zwerling was angling to tell his

Benjamin Franklin story and preferred to be out of earshot. The Founding Father was a fellow experimenter and the first user, as far as Mr. Zwerling was concerned, of the expression nor'easter. Mr. Zwerling read this account when he was in knee pants.

It seems Benjamin Franklin in Philadelphia received a letter from Boston remarking that a storm had passed on some such date. Franklin examined his weather calendar and saw that Philadelphia had been struck the following day. From this he deduced that the system had come from the northeast and he christened the storm a nor'easter. It was along those lines at least. It had been some time since Mr. Zwerling was in knee pants so the details were blurred.

"Now that's an intellect."

Benjamin Franklin's career in Paris also pleased Mr. Zwerling. Franklin was very popular and sought after by women.

"Quite the ladies man you know. You wouldn't think that, would you?"

It was not very cold for February though at eight in the morning the remaining Tenth Avenue street lights were still glowing. (Squeezed between the viaduct and the West Side Elevated Highway, the hardware store was often in shadows. Mr. Zwerling had long ago come to terms with the viaduct but the highway blocked the sunset from his windows.)

Mr. Zwerling was back on the sidewalk every few minutes. He wiped the rain from his glasses and redundantly wet his thumb. The wind was out of the south and he felt heavier drops on his forehead. A meat packer came down the street.

"Going to see Alphonse. Get you something?

"No, I got the pot on. Wind's picking up, don't you think?"

"Sure is."

Mr. Zwerling came out one last time with a thermometer. He shook it and stood at the corner. The thermometer read two degrees above freezing. Mr. Zwerling braced himself against the No Standing sign. The rain had turned to snow. The flakes were moist and heavy and they were sticking. He looked at the thermometer again.

"Funny," he said.

Mr. Zwerling turned the lights on in the store and turned the window sign to open. It was Sunday but someone might need something. In recent years he had reduced the cash register float to twenty dollars. It was three five dollar bills, three singles and the rest in coins. (Mr. Zwerling's father had removed the float before sundown on Fridays and put it in a baking soda can. If there were emergencies on the weekend he would open the store but would not accept any payment.)

"Come see me Monday," Mr. Zwerling senior said to them.

Emmett went to the basement and began bringing up premeasured bags of rock salt. (At the beginning of winter they kept a barrel of salt by the front door for their sidewalk and driveway. Neighborhood superintendents, tending their doorsteps, filled fire buckets from it.) Mr. Zwerling buttoned up his sweater and scribbled on a pad with his carpenter's pencil.

"How we fixed for windshield scrapers?"

He was thinking out loud. Emmett looked at the sky. It was getting harder to see. He drove the Silvercup van to the delicatessen on Ninth Avenue. Mr. Tomanelli was on the phone to Italy. He was telling his favorite sister that his son in the service was going to Germany and not Vietnam.

"I can sleep now," he said.

Emmett gave Mr. Tomanelli a bag of salt. He bought cold cuts, poppy seed rolls, milk and orange juice. The deli knew his hand signals. Mrs. Tomanelli did the slicing. She gave Emmett a thick slice of mortadella. Mr. Tomanelli was off the phone and peeling back the foil on a tray of macaroni and cheese.

"Looks like something, hun? All of a sudden this."

Emmett nodded. He pointed to the macaroni and cheese and Mr. Tomanelli filled two containers. "Don't forget the rice pudding," Mrs. Tomanelli said, "the girls like that."

Emmett added a string of frankfurters, baked beans, and three packs of Marlboros. The phone was ringing.

"We're open," Mr. Tomanelli said. "Why shouldn't we be open? You know something I don't? Go tell Hizzoner. That Lindsay. God help us."

"The radio said only rain," Mrs. Tomanelli said.

Mr. Tomanelli put the phone down. "They know nothing, like always."

He wrote the items down on a brown paper bag, added it up, and put a slip with the total underneath his change tray. Other customers were coming in. "Tell Mr. Z not to do any shoveling. I don't do it anymore."

When Emmett got back he heard the scrape of a shovel. While he was gone Mr. Zwerling gave out three bags of salt.

"Come see me tomorrow."

Mr. Zwerling told his Benjamin Franklin story three times. He was itching to get at that snow. (No knight in shining armor ever wanted at a dragon the way Mr. Zwerling wanted at that snow.) There was still rain mixed in. He shoveled the mash into the gutter to let it run down into the sewer. His breath was short. Emmett brought the groceries in and then came out and took the shovel away from Mr. Zwerling. He butted Mr. Zwerling in the backside with the shovel to urge him back into the store.

"All right already, I'm going, I'm going."

Mr. Zwerling was fifty-four and his arteries were not the best. This ran in his family. His father did not live to that age. Emmett finished the sidewalk, employing a more systematic method than Mr. Zwerling, and spread handfuls of salt. Emmett now assumed it would snow all day and into the night. It had that look.

The lights were still out on the top floor. Emmett heard Max come in late from the Tad's Steaks where she cleaned up the kitchen. (She was paid under the table and given leftover potatoes and garlic bread.) She was not looking forward to Monday when she had an appointment at Salome's school. What was called her daughter's lack of attentiveness was again to be discussed. These meetings were difficult for Max who felt out of place in the presence of teachers and other officials. Once, when Salome was in grade school, a social worker had been there who seemed to stare at Max as she wrote on a clipboard. Salome had been left back twice and it was doubtful, Max was notified, that she would ever graduate at her current rate of progress.

Max assumed it was her doing though she could not say when the mistakes began. Salome was shy away from home, away from the hardware store, and unable to communicate. She was, Max thought, dreamy and quiet the way some are.

"Far too dreamy and quiet," Max was told. "She needs to engage more."

By late afternoon the radio had changed its tune. They were calling it a snowstorm, originating from Virginia. This made no sense to Mr. Zwerling who wished the weather bureau would get its terminology straight.

"Can't have a nor'easter blowing up from Virginia. That's backwards I think."

He explained this several times to Emmett who nodded in agreement without enthusiasm. Before it was completely dark Emmett must check the roof. He took his snow shovel up the back stairs and knocked on Max's door. She and Salome were in bed under the covers. It was colder in the loft and Emmett sent them downstairs with their pillows and blankets. He went up through the hatchway. The wind was stronger. His concern was the weight of the wet, heavy snow.

From the rooftop, looking north and east at the meat-packing plants, Emmett saw that no matter what the storm was called it was a powerful one. He recalled how the tall metal windows of the foundling home rattled in the wind. One of the cooks there, her face was very red, made spaetzle and gave him extra portions when she could. She made it for her own children, she said. Emmett once went up to

Germantown to search for spaetzle like the cook made but none tasted the same.

The viaduct was shrouded. Emmett saw a light through the snow. A handcar was coming. It was Aaron, the only gandy dancer Emmett knew who was a colored man. Aaron had a lantern and smudge pots and was checking the tracks. Emmett kept a flashlight in his overalls. He clicked it on and held it above his shoulder.

Aaron laughed loudly. "That you, Emmett? You done white at last boy."

Emmett waved the flashlight. Aaron lived over in Jersey somewhere and had a family. "I hear they closed the airports," he shouted. "Cars are broken down every which way. Some mess. You get that work done and get out of this quick."

Emmett flashed his light twice as Aaron leaned down on the balance beam and disappeared along the track. Emmett shoveled snow off the roof until his back ached and he felt the sweat run inside his parka. He knew he would have a harder job in the morning.

Downstairs he checked the hutch he'd built in the driveway. It was behind the Silvercup van and under the lee of the viaduct, out of the rain though not of drifting snow. He built the enclosure for stray cats after Butch died. That was the store cat who kept the mice off. Butch had been twenty or thereabout and in her later years slept the day away inside a coil of hemp rope. That was Butch's corner and nothing else was kept there. Every morning Mr. Zwerling came in early to feed Butch and stroke her fur.

"That's a good worker. She earns her keep."

Mr. Zwerling chose not to replace Butch. Doesn't seem right, he said. He preferred not to watch another cat die. The mice came back and damaged various things.

"That's all right. Live and let live, I say, live and let live."

Paw prints ran from the open gate to the hutch and a dozen pairs of eyes were reflected in Emmett's flashlight glow. The cats were tucked in well enough. He'd changed the straw a few days earlier. There was an Entenmann's pie platter he filled with dry food. Some days he picked up offal and renderings from a meat packer and fed them outside the hutch. It brought more strays but they did not live long. They were often run down on Tenth Avenue though there were no longer any neighborhood boys to shoot at them with BB guns.

Emmett could make sounds with his lips to which some of the cats responded. He lost track of how many kittens he'd drowned in the horse trough. (Mr. Zwerling was not informed of this.) If their eyes were open he could not do it. He tried but he could not. Emmett went out to the sidewalk. A cat was huddled by the fire hydrant. It hissed. Emmett cleared a path to the hutch and opened the gate wider. The cat would come in when it came in. Emmett felt wet to the skin. He checked all the doors and went into the store. It was time to hunker down.

Mr. Zwerling and Max and Salome were playing Night Baseball. Mr. Zwerling learned the game from Joe Two-Axe though Joe Two-Axe called it something else. The circumstances called for the card table and a fresh deck of cards. Mr. Zwerling gave the deck to Salome and told her to do the honors. She peeled the cellophane off.

"They smell so nice."

In his bootlegging days Mr. Zwerling delivered growlers of Prohibition beer to card games in back rooms and betting parlors. He was pushed to the floor one night by a man objecting to the amount of foam. Another man picked him up and brushed him off and said the trick was to rub lard inside the rim of the growler. That kept the head down. The man winked and gave Mr. Zwerling a dollar.

"A dollar is good but it's more important to learn something."

Mr. Zwerling tapped the side of his nose to emphasize a statement. Salome looked up at Emmett. It was plain what she was thinking. There was a tradition during storms, they had done it the night of the blackout too. They had Dinty Moore beef stew. Emmett kept cans of it in his larder and served it to Salome with buttered white bread. The radio said drivers were trapped in their cars on the Tappan Zee Bridge.

"Never seen that bridge. Supposed to be a beauty."

Mr. Zwerling and Emmett ate frankfurters and baked beans. Max ate rice pudding and smoked Marlboros. Mr. Zwerling told his story of the one time he had tried chewing tobacco. It made him sick.

"Threw right up on my shoes."

Max had a memory of chewing tobacco she pushed to the back of her mind. She enjoyed the nights they spent in the store. It was a small excitement. The night of the blackout Butch slept with them on the wrestling mats Mr. Zwerling bought for these stayovers. Salome laughed because Butch was old and snored. Max had felt the cat's warmth at her back. It was years now since she'd had arms around her.

The wind was loud. Max was hopeful there would be no school the next day. It was a relief. Salome studied her cards, close to her face, with great concentration. She could be good at counting, unlike Scrabble or other board games. The school tested her hearing; at times her eyes had a faraway look. There were suggestions about cognitive skills but Max never learned what that was.

"She's happy," she said, "can't you see that?"

Emmett went down to stoke the furnace. Mr. Zwerling remembered he had not told Max and Salome about Benjamin Franklin. It was an excellent opportunity even if the radio had it all mixed up. That got Mr. Zwerling onto igloos, one of his favorite subjects. There was also the intriguing matter of ice fishing.

"Those people up there have it all figured out."

Emmett plugged a space heater in by the wrestling mats and set out a reading lamp. He checked the doors, wondering at the absence so far of snow plows. There should have been the sound of tire chains. It would not be an easy Monday. He waved good night and went to his room. After another hand Mr. Zwerling called it a night.

Emmett had purposely not shoveled the stairs outside. This kept Mr. Zwerling from climbing up to his floor. Mr. Zwerling doubled a wrestling mat behind the counter and slept on that, dreaming about barometers. Max and Salome went to bed.

Salome was sorry Butch was gone. Max switched on the reading light and read and smoked for an hour.

Mr. Zwerling was not a coffee drinker. He enjoyed, however, what he called the science of coffee preparation to the extent that most people could not drink the coffee he made. Max and Salome could. As soon as it was light Emmett went back to the roof to work. The train tracks on the viaduct were buried. The morning was very still and though the snow had stopped the air seemed frosted.

Emmett breathed in a crispness like pine needles. A hunger for the mountains was in him and he kept calendars in his room of the Andes and Rockies. He had great empathy for pack animals and other beasts of burden. He brought Mr. Zwerling's razor down to him. Mr. Zwerling could shave in the store's toilet. He did not care to be unshaven, to ever be seen so. Emmett indicated the depth of the snow, holding his hands apart about eighteen inches.

"Oy," Mr. Zwerling said, "oy vey. Not good."

Emmett made egg and cheese sandwiches for breakfast. Mr. Zwerling was not strict but he did not mix meat and dairy. They ate at the card table and listened to WNYC. The storm system had passed but left behind more snow than the region had experienced in eight years. Beginning on a Sunday, the blizzard had caught the city shorthanded. All schools were closed for the day and possibly for Tuesday as well. The subways were running.

"The subways never stop. You can count on that."

The Mayor had a press conference. There were charges of inadequate planning. There was still very little snow removal equipment on the road. The radio said the Sanitation Department was hiring to help clear sidewalks and crosswalks. They were paying $2.50 per hour and the work was expected to be available for three days. Max went upstairs for her overcoat and snow boots. Mr. Zwerling tried to stop her but she said it would be good exercise. As much as Mr. Zwerling, Emmett understood that she did what she wanted to do.

There was a Sanitation Department garage on Spring Street. Max's boots sank deep into the snow. It was easier walking under the elevated highway where the drifts were not as high. There were abandoned cars and mounds of trash beside the No Dumping signs. The wind gusts shook the framework of the Cunard pier. The pier was abandoned when the transatlantic liners stopped running.

It was more than a mile to the garage and Max was winded when she reached the group of men standing at the West Street corner. The line stretched around to the Spring Street side. There were salt trucks lined up at each angle of the intersection. Pan shovels were distributed to the men who had registered. A bus was waiting to take them to Eighth Avenue. Several men made way for Max. The supervisor saw her.

"Lady, please, this is not for you, take my word for it."

"I'm strong," Max said, "I can work."

"Sweetheart, this stuff weighs a ton. I'd rather give you ten bucks from my pocket than have you die out here on me. You'd be on my conscience for God's sake."

"I need…"

"Lady, I'm asking you, please. Don't make my day any worse than it is now."

The supervisor turned away from her and asked a man in line for his name. There were no other women there. Walking down Tenth Avenue, Max had spent in her mind the money she might have earned. Clothes for Salome, even shoes, something for her sixteenth birthday. That was next month.

That day in March in 1953 had been cold like this one. Max lay in a ward at St. Vincent's and Emmett was in the waiting room with a crossword puzzle book. The nurse asked if Emmett was the father. Max did not say yes, she did not say no. In the hospital it did not seem so strange but on Tenth Avenue it was shocking to have a child. By that time she was used to the viaduct but when the train passed and her breast jiggled as she was nursing she had to laugh. It seemed so funny.

"She's just slow," a teacher said to Max, "some children are like that."

The snow had turned to slush in some places and Max fell crossing Houston Street, bruising her hand. As she tried to rise she felt her feet were in quicksand as flurries flew around her. She was sorry to think she could not have worked for very long.

Up ahead she saw Mr. Zwerling outside. He was at the hotel, holding the blanket from his wrestling mat bed. At the hardware store they called it the hotel or the Sailor's Rest. Mr. Zwerling's father had said the Sailor's Rest because he thought the word whorehouse was unkind, a mean thing to say about people. As there were no sailors any longer they now mostly said hotel.

An ambulance was stuck at the Fourteenth Street corner. Emmett and the driver were digging around the wheels. A police car was behind the ambulance. Two policemen got out and crossed to the hotel on foot. A window above them opened and a man leaned through it.

"She doesn't belong here."

A woman wearing a white slip was crumpled in the snow. One strap had fallen and was frozen to her shoulder. There were ice crystals in her hair. Mr. Zwerling covered her with his blanket. Emmett had gone into the store for sand and cardboard boxes. Once the ambulance had traction they pushed it across the street. One policeman leaned over the woman and put his hand to her neck.

"This is wrong," Mr. Zwerling said. "This shouldn't happen."

A stretcher was brought from the ambulance. The driver was slipping in the snow. Don't knock yourself out, the policeman said, there's no rush. Mr. Zwerling did not have a coat on and one side of his face was shaved. Emmett took his arm but Mr. Zwerling pulled away. He shouted up at the hotel.

"Do you hear what I'm saying? Do you? God is watching. This is a person here, a human being. This shouldn't happen to anyone."

Mr. Swerling was wearing the vest he used at the counter, with the pockets for his eyeglasses and his carpenter's pencil. Max put her arm around his waist. He gave in and she led him across the street to the hardware store.

1955

Max picked up her copies of the *Village Voice* on Wednesday mornings. The promised canvas carrier bags had not arrived but she had borrowed one from an old newsboy who did his drinking at Jack Delaney's most nights. His name was Hoppy, due to an injury caused by a Herald Square streetcar on Armistice Day. *The World* (New York) was stamped on the bag. It was stained and the strap well worn but in her newsboy cap from the army-navy store Max felt officially outfitted.

The *Voice* office was on Greenwich Avenue at Tenth Street and she was there before the other newshawks. The trick was to catch the early birds at the coffee houses. The weekly paper was a nickel and a year's subscription was two dollars. (She kept the subscription book in her newsboy cap with a cartridge pen and her Marlboros.)

The paper's circulation manager, who was also an editor and answered the phone, suggested after Thanksgiving that Max emphasize giving subscriptions as Christmas presents. They'd come up with a card, secular, where the name of the recipient and the giver could be written in a non-denominational winter setting. (The *Voice* was new and they were working to get the word out widely.)

It said Season's Greetings, which was a relief to Max who never did learn to pronounce Hanukkah very well. (Her first sale was Mr. Zwerling who maintained the subscription for the rest of his life. Like Social Security, he believed he had gotten in on the ground floor of something.)

"They'll think of you every week when they go to the mailbox."

Max rehearsed that. She was using the pea coat she'd acquired when pregnant. She liked the way it buttoned. It was a men's 38, allowing at the time for her expanded belly. Some of that weight never came off and with a sweater under it the coat was really not too big for her. There was an anchor stitched on one sleeve and a name written on the inner lining. The name was too faded to read and she was glad of that, afraid she would think of that man and wonder who he was and if he was still a sailor. (It was wondering about people that got you in hot water, that got you in the drink.)

She saw them on the piers when the ships came in and they looked at times so unsettled. (When they went ashore it was onto Tenth Avenue and it was cobblestones.) They have sea legs, Mr. Zwerling said, you can tell by their walk. Max supposed she had farm legs. She approached the thick wooden turnstiles on the subway as if they were stud bulls.

Mr. Zwerling had a broad acquaintance amongst gadgets and job lot overstock. (Better a white elephant than a pink one, he said.) When Max said she would be a newsboy he went to the basement and rummaged in his storage crates and barrels. He was searching for a coin changer though other items that turned up distracted him. (Even Mr. Zwerling did not deny that he was easily distracted.)

"Didn't know I still had that."

He found the coin changer wrapped in gauze cloth. It was inside a Dutch oven filled with nuts and bolts. A Bungalow Bar man had dropped it off though Mr. Zwerling did not remember why. A change apron might have been simpler but he was drawn more often than not to the mechanical.

"Nickel plated, four-barrelled, good workmanship."

The dime dispenser stuck a bit but Max was very pleased. This made up somewhat for the failure of his baby carriage. After Salome was born he pursued several designs meant to combine lightweight convenience, durability, and sufficient suspension to withstand the ever-present Belgian paving blocks. (He had grown up with the rumble of those streets and had to admit that even trucks were quieter than horse drawn wagons.)

Sketches were spread out on the store's counter for months but one obstacle after another arose and he was increasingly stymied by the inclusion of a shopping basket under the wheels. It just did not come together and at one point Max hinted that she did not think a baby carriage would be helpful.

"That's a consideration."

Emmett was busy with another idea. On his visits to the Indian museum he saw the cradleboards American tribes used. They were various. Emmett was not a weaver (though the weavings at the museum made him want to take it up) but he built a birch wood frame with a footrest and a canopy. It was lined with rabbit fur and he extended the frame twice as Salome grew. When her daughter began walking Max used the cradleboard less but on her *Village Voice* days she wanted Salome with her.

In her pea coat with Salome on her back and the *World* bag at her side, Max became *The Papoose Girl of Bleecker and MacDougal.* The *Voice* photographer took her picture and she appeared on the third page of one issue holding the paper high above Salome's head.

"Read all about it."

On Sixth Avenue Max passed Miss Svenson, a teacher, whom she would not encounter again for seventeen years. (Miss Svenson had an interview at The Little Red Schoolhouse. It was fought to a draw. They thought Miss Svenson too stiff; she found the facility undisciplined. She chose to remain in the public school system.)

The day was sunny and Max was not tired. She never felt so when she was out with Salome. (The kinetic energy of Salome's growth seemed to propel Max from behind.) She picked up more papers at the *Voice* office and then recrossed Sixth Avenue and went into Bigelow's drugstore. She'd developed regulars there and the store smelled like wax and flowers, like vitamins. The druggist gave Salome a lollipop and Max drank a coffee standing up at the counter. She sold three papers. One man gave her a quarter and she needed to hit the plunger four times to give him two dimes. (Mr. Zwerling said he would look at it.)

Because the Dodgers had won the World Series a *Daily News* headline was taped to the side of the cash register. All the newsstands had sold out that day and the day after.

"I can't fill that. Don't come in here again."

The druggist was talking to a boy with a piece of paper. The boy fingered the paper. It was dirty and torn at one edge.

"I need it," the boy said. He was coughing.

"I can't help you."

The druggist put his hand on the telephone. It was a threat and the boy left. Max finished her coffee and looked at the perfume showcase. There was a special on Evening in Paris but she did not like it. She found it too smoky. Two favorites, Cocktail Dry and Jean Patou, were there. It would be thrilling to have one for Christmas. She imagined a small package with wrapping and a red ribbon in front of her door. (In the days when she mucked out the stall she washed herself at the pump with lye soap. That was for eating, she did not mind any of the smells.)

She wouldn't open the package right away but look at it from time to time and try to guess. It could even be earrings. It must be wonderful, she sometimes thought, to be given earrings. Max drank her coffee black. (Even Mr. Zwerling's coffee.) She poured the milk provided into Salome's bottle and went outside.

The sun was bright. She went south on the east side of the avenue. As she passed the fruit stand the fruitmonger gave her a handful of dried cherries. He made them every fall. She stopped at Eighth Street and sold two papers at the corner. That's when Tony came out of the Waldorf cafeteria, slouching. He looked underweight and haggard. She had seen him the year before by accident. (It must be by accident; she would not seek him out, she couldn't.) He was flush at that moment, wearing clean clothes that fit and smoking a Di Nobili.

A gallery then had given Tony a stipend and for three months he was productive. After that it was more pleasant to sit around and shoot the breeze, though those to whom he now spoke were not other artists. The old meeting places had changed (because art movements age more quickly than children) and the parties were fewer. At that time he was living on St. Mark's Place with a girl he described as a rich Jew type. She talked to him about Carl Jung until he was about to scream.

"She's slumming," Tony said, "be out the door soon, scram, vamoose, going, going, gone, pffft."

He wasn't wrong about that but he bragged he could read people like a book. (This was opposed to reading a real book, something he did not do.) He asked Max if she knew her portrait had been sold. When she was six months pregnant she ran into Elaine who decided she'd do a madonna.

"Just for a study," she said, "not really in my line."

Max sat for her for two weeks in Carmine Street. It was cold and she was naked. (Posing for a woman was fine and she loved to show off her convex abdomen.) The baby heat helped and Elaine boiled water on the stove. When the phone rang Max put on Elaine's bathrobe while waiting. She was in a chair, her legs slightly apart, her navel protruding, her breasts spilling down. Tony had seen it and said it was not bad.

"But I'm not a painter so who can say."

Tony believed his opinion was sought by all. He gave advice to the men digging Con Edison holes in the street and to the barber cutting his hair.

"Who went to school for this, buddy, you or me?"

Tony was not manic that day, only a little buoyant, like a cup of good joe in the morning or one drink at five o'clock.

"Imagine your twat above somebody's fireplace like that. Funny, I guess."

The Jewish girl on St. Mark's Place was an egghead and could not boil water. Tony preferred the more down to earth type but girls get ruined pretty quick. (What ruins men comes straight on, Margaret said, girls get it every which way.)

Some joker tells them they're smart and the next thing they're looking over your shoulder. Tony twisted his head at that and blamed it on the war. That loused it all up, he said, and the goddamn French were to blame.

"Don't you think?"

He went off, in a puff of cigar smoke, without waiting for an answer or asking for money. She'd been relieved. That was then. Seeing Tony now, Max backed up into a doorway. The cut of his body, his head turned sideways, said there was no longer any Jewish girl and probably no St. Mark's Place either. There might be a park bench and the public baths. The austerity was on him like a hard frost and with Salome behind her Max was afraid.

He might follow her home and want to talk about Weehawken Street and everything that can no longer be. (That is the hardest thing. When someone looks you in the eye and talks about what is no more. And he might give her news of Jack.) Sometimes he remembered Weehawken Street. He had illuminations like sunspots and they gave him migraines.

Tony leaned on a car fender. Max guessed he did not have fifteen cents in his pocket. She was biting her lips against the impulse to cross the street and speak to him. He raised his head, as if remembering something, and lurched into the cafeteria again. It was his kidneys and an unconscious kindness on his part.

Max looked in a bank window for the time. It was half-past ten. She'd tried twice to get work in a bank but it was the same thing again and again. Those things she could not do. She had dreamed of working in a bank and having five days of clothing she could take to the dry cleaners. (There was a woman on Bethune Street who did day babysitting. She did not cost much but said she did not take mixed children. She did not mind herself, she said, but it was a problem for some of the mothers.)

Salome needed to be changed. Max hurried down Sixth Avenue to Bleecker and turned left towards the Figaro.

The morning woman there was Italian and did not mind if Max used the WC for Salome. She'd wait outside the door while mother and daughter were inside, guarding the cradleboard. She had a gold tooth and never failed to have a broken cannoli to slip in Max's coat.

Max washed her hands and came out and sold a subscription to a man looking at the *Voice* at a table. The Figaro, the Borgia, and the Reggio cafes had taken the paper for a year. (The Peacock had not.) They kept them on their newspaper racks.

When Max saw someone reading the *Voice* she went up to them and talked about it.

"They'll think of you when they go to the mailbox."

She went across the street to the Borgia. She was hoping to see someone. He was often there at this time, sitting alone with a book or writing on a pad. He kept his coat on with a scarf loosely tied around his neck. There was an espresso cup and foreign cigarettes and a box of Smith Brothers wild cherry cough drops beside his hand. He had thick black hair, combed back straight.

Max wondered that she liked that. When she was a girl all the boys were fair haired and pale and some of them giggled like girls. (Some of the giggles were directed her way because she developed early.) She did not like that. Margaret liked to say that the men in your life were telephone poles on the highway. They were more or less evenly spaced and a little monotonous. Sometimes Margaret looked at the Wanted Posters in the post office for the sake of variety. A good deep facial scar held her attention more than Mona Lisa's smile did.

"Vicious, maybe amoral, but never boring. Too bad he's on the lam." (At the unemployment office Margaret sometimes replied gun moll when asked about her former occupation. One man asked her how to spell moll.)

Max hoped to find the good looking student at the Borgia reading the *Voice* but he did not seem to read the papers, only books. She did not know who Rilke was though Camus was famil-iar. (She had passed through or walked around conversations about writers and artists where people said you're wrong about that, you make no sense, you have no idea what you're talking about. She was sorry not to learn something, anything at all.)

The man reading had a graceful shadow of a beard like a longshoreman or someone playing a pirate. She did not know anyone well enough at the Borgia to ask who he was. It was darker there than across the street. She'd heard the Figaro was for tourists and to pick up girls. The Borgia was quieter and men read the Italian newspapers and played chess. The espresso machine seemed very old like a polished antique and when the light changed in the afternoon it shone like a fountain in the sunlight.

"I have a complaint."

Someone tapped her shoulder. She did not remember him. The *Voice* carried an ad for Fish and Cheeps, a pet store on Second Avenue. They sold singing canaries. The man had bought two canaries as a present for his wife who was not agreeably disposed. He did not mind saying he had purchased the canaries in hope of pacifying his wife so he could read the newspaper in peace. These canaries did not sing, not a peep, and his wife was grumpier than ever. What did she (Max, not his wife) intend to do about it? Max did not know.

"Am I supposed to go to the Canary Islands for better canaries?"

The man had prepared this triumphant statement. That's how you won an argument with a haymaker like that. It was all in the delivery. The man who was reading Rilke looked up from his table. He put a cherry cough drop in his mouth and fixed it with his tongue.

"Actually," he said, "the Canary Islands are named for the wild dogs that were prevalent there. From the Latin *canis* for dog. The name has nothing to do with birds. Your misapprehension is a common one."

"Says who?"

"Pliny the Elder."

The man with the unhappy wife laughed haughtily, disbelieving. The younger man stood up. He tightened his scarf and put his books under his arm. He put his cigarettes and Smith Brothers cough drops in his pocket. He took out a blue watch cap and pulled it down over his ears. Max was sorry to see that beautiful hair covered up.

"If you'll excuse me," he said, "I have a class."

He left. Max never saw him again and she gave the man who bought the canaries his nickel back.

1998

They let Salome go at the Salvation Army on a Wednesday. There was a small party with tea and Hostess cupcakes and a gift box of chocolates from Barracini. For Salome the party was an afterthought. Lorraine was retiring after thirty years of riding the F train in from Queens and not missing a day. Most of her co-workers hoped she would miss a day now and then but Lorraine disappointed them with her exceptional regularity.

As file clerks go she was efficiency itself, reminding many of a paper clip, invisible much of the time but so very useful in a pinch. Tacking Salome onto the departure of Lorraine, killing two birds with one stone as it were, was deemed a masterstroke. It was thought Salome would catch on more quickly if there were two of them on the way out. Lorraine was briefly offended but realized that Salome was unlikely to steal the limelight.

Given the right task, Salome was efficient too. She looked forward to those times of the year when there were mailings and she sealed envelopes for hours. (She might be reprimanded for licking them and not using the sponge. She liked licking them and thought the sponge was awful. It was. She likely as a child licked many things she should not have.) She was slow at the Pitney Bowes postage meter but that too was enjoyable as the envelopes piled up in the post office bin.

Lorraine did not at first believe the rumors. Reorganization was one thing but this talk of computerization was idiotic. Hints were dropped. You can't teach an old horse new tricks, she heard someone say. She supposed there were old horses around to be put out to pasture but that was the nature of business. The Salvation Army was not a business of course but the principle was the same.

Still it was a surprise when she was invited to leave and kindly comments such as you won't have to take the F train anymore did not help. (Well, Lorraine liked the F train. The cars were still newish and since air conditioning came in she barely noticed the ride. And this talk of doing away with the token was only that, talk, cheap talk.) Yet before long she was resigned. The neighborhood had changed and shopping was not what it once was. (Klein's On the Square was long gone and you took your life in your hands walking through that park.)

She was miffed though when told that Salome would be leaving too and given the same cupcake. It appeared to place them on the same level, which was obviously wrong. There was something not quite right with that girl. Sweet enough, undemonstrative, but a little too much in her own world. Calling her a file clerk was a little ridiculous but that was the Salvation Army for you, erring somehow on the wrong side of charity.

The party was not a success, the cupcakes were stale, and the disappointment Lorraine experienced when she was not taken to lunch at the Dardanelles (a spontaneous idea of her own, she was fond of shish kebab) never lifted. It was a trial being polite to people not sorry to see her go. (She knew they weren't, she could tell.) She'd put on more makeup than normal and felt foolish. Someone asked if she had plans for later on. No, no plans at all. She did not know what she would do if she did not get up and ride the F train.

She liked the *Today* show, it was often educational, and she'd typically caught a few minutes of it before walking to the station. Now she could watch it all and leave the television on until the soap operas began. Don't start watching soap operas, someone said. Lorraine found that unnecessarily brutal, the insinuation that she had nothing better to do.

But it had all been brutal, hadn't it, from start to finish. She could not recall the last time someone asked about herself, how the weekend was or if the dress she wore was new. They never asked if she was coming down with something or been to the hairdresser or if she liked Thai food. (She didn't). She inquired, she complimented, she agreed, she spent the most on the Christmas grab bag. (Secret Santa was a blessing for penny pinchers.) She saved for months for an orchestra seat to *Les Miserables,* a Saturday matinee. She brought the *Playbill* in on Monday morning and put it on her desk. No one mentioned it.

Only Salome, the last person you would expect, stared at the *Playbill* cover and then oddly, very oddly, touched the picture of the girl with her finger and held it there. Lorraine was tempted to say that this was Cosette, to tell her the story, but what was the point? Salome never seemed to understand what was said to her if it was not about stuffing envelopes or hanging holiday decorations.

Lorraine was told she could leave early, beat rush hour, get a seat on the blasted F train wrenching her to Queens for the last time. It was as if they could not wait to see her gone and have the East River between them finally, once and for all. They were clearing away the cupcake crumbs and washing the cups. Lorraine wanted to help but was quietly led aside. Really, no one expected her to do that on her special day. On the subway platform Lorraine stood against the tiled wall sobbing.

"Oh my God in heaven."

When the big guns gathered, when the big chiefs were there for a confab, someone was bound to ask: who's walking the plank today? Lorraine had walked the plank.

The plan appeared to have backfired when Salome came to work Thursday morning. There was some confusion until she was told firmly that she did not work there anymore. She was gently shown out but came back again on Friday. This was exasperating. It was decided to send someone home with Salome to talk to her family.

As no one volunteered, Grady was told to do it. He wasn't pleased and even less so when given Salome's address. The thought of Tenth Avenue disturbed him. He had no idea what might be over there. The Salvation Army was between Sixth and Seventh Avenues, in a building so resembling a fortress it was called that. In a few minutes, walking east, you were on Fifth Avenue, the Gold Coast. (Where he slipped quietly into the East-West bookstore to read a bit of Alan Watts or Gurdjieff and look at girls. Grady had his hidden ecumenical side.) You could trust Fifth Avenue.

Tenth Avenue was the other way, the other path so to speak, but he hadn't any choice. Grady was somewhat on probation and these Job-like persecutions must be endured. There was that day in divinity school in the remote past. He was on Riverside Drive and felt a sudden urge. He flagged a passing taxi.

"I want to have fun."

"All right," the cab driver said.

Grady was taken to CBGB on Bowery where his black suit and ministerial tie seemed at home. He drank shooters chased with Pabst Blue Ribbon and learned some of the lyrics of "Too Drunk to Fuck." It was remarkably easy, he found, to climb atop a bar and dance if you were called on to do so. (He had been subject to calls since adolescence.) Grady was found the next morning in the courtyard of his residence hall in his Jockey shorts, clutching a Dead Kennedys tee shirt and whispering the name Laura.

Salome, once on the sidewalk, walked forthrightly and quickly. Grady was surprised. At the office she seemed so sluggish. He nearly had to trot to keep up with her. Once they passed Ninth Avenue his misgivings grew. There was a smell, he could not place it. Several men passed whose aprons were smeared with blood. Part of the street was desolate and many of the buildings that had been meat packing plants showed broken windows and rampant graffiti.

Salome stopped at the Tenth Avenue corner and opened a wooden gate. It scraped the concrete. Inside the driveway Grady saw a Silvercup van with missing tires. The hood was up and the engine had been stripped. There was an odor of cats or something worse. Salome pointed to a rickety staircase. It did not appear safe to him, not at all. And they were under what looked like a railroad. He had never seen it before. There was ivy hanging down, nearly brushing his head.

"Sweet potato vines," Salome said, smiling.

Grady felt she had a good smile though several teeth were missing. A girl came across the street. She had a slow walk, but not hesitant, a little provocative. She was the spunky type, a source of temptation to acolytes since the world began God knows. Grady said good morning in his gracious, clerical way. She said her name was Tiff and kickily offered to suck his big white cock for twenty dollars. He stood wordless, not knowing what to say. The girl would skedaddle when she understood he was not what she had taken him for.

"How about fifteen?"

This was not good. It was one thing to politely decline the overtures of a streetwalker. That could happen to anyone but now he appeared to be bargaining with her. Grady looked nervously along the street. He expected to see a photographer approaching. That was how they got you.

The previous year Grady was told to evaluate prospective sidewalk Santas for the holidays. He could not fathom why he was given this job. In his view the men were a bunch of old boozers and one was more or less like another. If they could stand up straight, or nearly, he hired them.

Unfortunately, one troublemaker, named Bob, slipped through Grady's careful grilling. ("Like working outdoors? Do you own socks? Any communicable diseases?") Bob was placed near the entrance to the Brooklyn-Battery Tunnel (Manhattan side) and the fumes made him weepy. Not long before Christmas a sympathetic motorist gave Bob a pint of Mogen David to cheer him up. The wine went to Bob's head and his loins.

"It's so nice out," he said, "I think I'll keep it out."

Bob was arrested for exposing himself to a school bus. That carries multiple counts. A New York *Post* reporter was in the vicinity with a camera. The front page headline for the following day was in large boldface type. It said simply: SAINT DICK. Grady was called in for a talk and told to shape up.

Tiff leaned closer to him. "You know you want it."

Of course, there were times when he wished to be taunted. It was only natural in missionary work. Tiff's purple fingernails were slightly shorter than those of Nosferatu or a Chinese mandarin. He breathed through his teeth, sensing the heavy scent of humiliation. He could foresee her nails beginning behind his ear and dragging towards his chin like a straightedge. If she drew blood he would be lost but suddenly, thankfully, he remembered it was Good Friday.

"I know my Redeemer liveth," he said.

Assuming he had done his duty by Salome, Grady turned and ran. He supposed they were testing him and this time at least he had not succumbed.

"You got a bathroom?"

Salome nodded. Tiff followed her up the staircase. Some of the steps had rotted away and Tiff braced her hand on the side of the building. In the loft Salome pointed. Tiff went into the water closet. It was springtime but she thought it was the coldest toilet she had ever sat on. The de Kooning on the inside of the door stared at her. Outside, when she had finished, she looked around at the walls.

"You got some funny pictures."

Salome laughed a little. She had never known any other room but this small museum. It sounded funny to hear them mentioned out loud like this. Those were the colors the walls were painted.

Tiff examined her. "You black?"

"I guess so, maybe."

Tiff admitted to sucking some crazy johnson in her day but this girl was out there. "You got any beer?"

Salome didn't. The refrigerator no longer worked. She was using the refrigerator in Emmett's old room downstairs. She had drunk all the root beer he'd left behind. Tiff examined the paint covered coffee cans. There was no dust. Salome cleaned every morning as her mother had. Tiff gave up. There did not seem to be anything worth stealing. (She did not use a lot, a little chipping now and then, some crack. Nothing serious.) There was a typewriter but you couldn't get anything for them these days. She walked up and down in front of the Pollock wall, sticking her nail into a nodule of paint.

"That's some ugly. You know that?"

Salome struggled to recall the word her mother had used. "Impasto," she said.

Tiff didn't hear her. She was thinking she was not making any money standing there yakking. "You got nobody here with you?"

Salome said she did not. She was beginning to forget how long it had been. There was the way it was and then there was the rest. Tiff went to the doorway.

"Okay, you take care now baby girl."

It was odd to hear other steps on the staircase. Salome straightened the coffee cans Tiff had moved. There was an order to them, the same order that had long prevailed. When her mother got sick it was frightening at first. Max could walk but she was unsteady. She often fell in the dark. One night she swept all the coffee cans from their shelf as she tried to break her fall.

The matchbooks, the pens and pencils and buttons, the few nickels and dimes spilled to the floor. Her mother could not put it right. She moaned as Salome lifted her up. It was harder after that, those years, but it was better because there was no hope.

Salome put her last check from the Salvation Army in a coffee can. There were two others. She brought her checks to Alphonse at the Square Meal who cashed them for her at his check cashing. He also paid the Con Edison bill that was still delivered to the hardware store. It was in Mr. Zwerling's name.

Alphonse did not charge for these services. (Max in her day had overtipped the waitresses and listened to Alphonse talk about his daughter with muscular dystrophy. She had also kept his secret.) Salome's wages came back to her inside the Con Edison return payment envelope. The money went in another coffee can.

Since Tomarelli's closed Salome found shopping more difficult. The larger stores made her anxious. (The Food Emporium was the scariest.) She often bought one item, Ritz crackers or licorice or packaged bologna. It was easier that way. Yogurt was a great discovery. It filled her up and was a little bit sweet. She tried different flavors in rotation before returning to plain. The plain yogurt was not as nice but it was there and had to be eaten before she could go on to the next kind.

It was only recently that Salome had begun to search through garbage cans. After leaving work one afternoon she waited for the light to cross Eighth Avenue. The city trash receptacle near her was overflowing and there was a bag from McDonald's on top. She saw French fries inside it. When she got home she found part of a hamburger. It was so easy and did not require any talking or counting change or feeling looked at. After that she had a pattern of reconnaissance and discovered things she had never eaten before.

Salome emptied the rain buckets. The roof leaked and it had showered overnight. She mopped the floor and opened the windows. It would be weeks perhaps before the warmer air penetrated the loft. Max had never wanted house plants. (They made her sad, the way a few things did.) She used to tell a story about a man who bought a canary that did not sing. It made Salome laugh, the way Max imitated the man. Mr. Zwerling once gave her an ant farm, which fascinated Salome until it fell and broke from the train vibrations.

Salome liked insects. She liked worms and the feel of dirt. She had brought up all the potting soil and vermiculite in the hardware store to the loft. The bags went on her head and she carried them up the ladder to the roof and across the staging planks to the viaduct. It took many months but like her mother she enjoyed a project. The tracks were covered from the Nabisco Building to Little West 12th Street. Mr. Zwerling never sold many seed packets. (The Burpee catalog, however, was some of his favorite reading.) There were boxes of them in the basement where the rats had got at them.

Salome spread handfuls of anonymous seeds up and down the viaduct. Now that spring had come, there would be golden-rod and cabbages. She did not know what else. Surprises could be very nice and nature decides. (Unlike the schoolyard where so much else intervenes between girls and boys.) There might be rhododendrons and cucumbers and more vines snaking through the railway ties. Salome made trellises from chicken wire and took apart the duck blind Emmet once made for her. She reas-sembled it on the tracks. Emmett bought rabbits and guinea pigs before he left. (She never knew why he did not say goodbye.) A meat packer gave her Muscovy ducks he raised in the Bronx. She hoped for a rooster someday to awaken her at dawn.

Salome climbed the ladder and stepped on the roof. It was breezy and the tarpulin she'd laid across parts of the tar paper was rippling. It had been a nice day. She'd had a visitor and Grady had walked with her along the street. (Grady was good to her. He gave her Lifesavers and Necco wafers and ran for the first aid kit when she stapled herself. When the peroxide stung he softly patted the sting away.)

She understood now why they no longer wanted her. There were no more envelopes. She had sealed them all. When some-thing was done, Max said, it was done. Now there would be more time for the garden. Salome skipped across the middle staging plank onto the viaduct. She waved to the osprey stand. They had come early this year, even before Salome had time to worry. The female raised a hesitant wing but, recognizing Salome, resumed her nesting. There was a scurrying in the grass and a pair of eyes came forward to her feet and then another and another. She was home. Salome reached her arms to the sky. She was in Eden.

1977

Max had two apartments she cleaned in Westbeth. There was also a house on Jane Street. The house was the simplest because Miss Bascom used only the parlor floor and did not have much furniture. Max did her shopping, which was a pleasure, and washed her clothes. (Max thought she had the most delicate underwear she had ever seen. Her own underwear was coarse and frayed.)

Miss Bascom had been in the silent movies. A few friends came some nights to drink a glass of sherry and reminicse. Sometimes they recreated scenes from the films they had been in together. On the night of the blackout, it was very warm and humid, two of them could not go home and had to sleep on the floor. Max found them the next morning cheerfully waiting for the electricity to come back on. We're actors, they told her, we can sleep anywhere. One said he would teach her a buck and wing but she did not feel up to it right then.

At Westbeth she cleaned for Miss Hooper and Crookshank. Miss Hooper was a writer and was away for the summer. Max watered her plants and dusted and tried to earn the reduced wage Miss Hooper provided when she was out of the country. Miss Hooper had hundreds of books and it was difficult not to take one out and read for a few minutes by the window. (It was there Max discovered Flannery O'Connor and Eudora Welty.) Crookshank, by contrast, was an artist. She had gone by that name for many years, since the 1930's, and did not care to be called anything else.

"Crookshank, please, no ifs, ands, or buts."

Both Miss Hooper and Crookshank had been among the first residents at Westbeth. (The disused Bell Telephone Laboratory buildings became an artists community. It was a short walk down West Street for Max. On the Washington Street side the viaduct ran through it.)

The two ladies were not chummy to any degree though this was expressed differently. Miss Hooper mostly ignored Crookshank while Crookshank could not stop talking, complaining really, about Miss Hooper. Part of it had to do with money, of which Miss Hooper had a good amount while Crookshank had very little.

"Subsidized housing in the winter and the south of France in the summer. Now does that sound fair to you? Hosted and toasted from one villa to another like a mediocre Fitzgerald character with the mark of Trotsky on her snoot all the while. Bah!"

Another contention between the two, at least on Crookshank's side, was politics as the Trotsky reference possibly indicates. Crookshank was often a bit peppy after an issue of *The Nation* or *The New York Review of Books*, which she read at her kitchen table while smoking Chesterfields, chewing Tums, and drinking instant coffee. Her hair was brick red, one of the dominant colors in her earlier work, and after a hot bath she plucked her bristly eyebrows with needle nose pliers. At home she wore pedal pushers and sweatshirts stiff with sweat, sealant, and acrylic.

"Miss Crookshank: should I do the drapes today?"

"How many times do I have to tell you? It's Crookshank, plain and simple. For God's sake, do I look like a Miss to you?"

Max almost said no ma'am but caught herself in time. (Ma'am was not permitted either, a childhood usage difficult for Max to discontinue.) Crookshank owed for three weeks. If she was in a sufficiently sour mood she was given to say: don't bother me about that now. Max answered an ad in the *Village Voice* that Miss Hooper had placed. When Crookshank saw her taking out Miss Hooper's trash one day she shouted down the stairs.

"What do you charge for that sort of thing?"

"Three dollars an hour..." Max didn't like to ask for carfare as she did not need it but in recent weeks she'd felt a strange weakness in her legs. "And carfare."

Crookshank seemed to find this a bit rich for her blood. She explained that her rooms were spotlessly clean and required only the lightest caress with a chamois. This was in contrast to her most recent paramour (it was not all that recent) who described her bedroom as looking like a dog's breakfast. Crookshank painted in the living room (it had better though not especially good light), which resembled not so much a dog's breakfast as the interior of a forgotten burlesque house. (Careful where you sit down, said the former paramour.)

Crookshank rarely discarded anything connected to her work and it was this, she insisted, that gave her apartment a charming atelier look. (How often had she dreamed of Picasso's *Bateau Lavoir* and the commune of creation?) She offered Max two dollars an hour without carfare and then they would see. Max said yes and her first assignment was the Venetian blinds, gummy and as yellow as old piano keys. (She scrubbed the blinds in the bathtub though she had to scrub the bathtub first.) Max's chambray shirtfront was wet and her Playtex gloves were dripping when Crookshank told her to go down for the mail and to get some skim milk as long as she was out anyway.

"Instant coffee is intolerable without it..."

Crookshank considered Westbeth to be off the beaten track. When she was awarded the apartment years earlier, she was living at the Chelsea Hotel. (She'd been in residence there for some time.) Her hotel room did not have a kitchen but she'd been eating in cafeterias since her art school days and preferred it to cooking on her own.

Her favorite cafeteria was Dubrow's in the garment district where she had kasha varnishkes (heavily sauced with ketchup and Tabasco) and seltzer for lunch several days a week amid the schmoozing of salesmen and fabric cutters. A discarded copy of *The Daily Worker* or another communist publication was to be expected, giving her something additional to chew on. She was a habitue there, as she was in the lobby of the Chelsea where she had a painting on the wall. (There was another above the staircase between the second and third floors.)

She got on well with Mr. Bard, the manager, and other long term guests, some of whom she knew from former left wing circles. It was cozy. Revisionists and other backsliders sometimes passed through but the hotel atmosphere was in general pleasantly Stalinist enough for her. (Crookshank liked a hard line, she liked borders; this was evident in her paintings.)

As for supper she had something from a can in her room, often deviled ham on crackers or Vienna sausage. To celebrate (such as good news from her dealer) she went to Keen's Chop House and had a strip steak and two Manhattans. (She disliked being waited on by women, there was more and more of this, but Keen's was holding the line.) That was to her liking. A solid meal out and a grappa afterwards left her at peace with all except her younger sister who lived in a split bedroom on West End Avenue and specialized in cosmetic surgery. Her sister had burned through three husbands, had grown richer with each divorce, and refused to call her Crookshank.

"It's a ridiculous name, Emmeline, surely you must realize that?"

It was supposed to have been Hotspur but that was taken by a cartoonist for the Hearst papers and Hotspur (the original that is) was probably a reactionary. (But then Prince Hal was hardly a Bolshevik.) Several times a year Crookshank broke bread with her sister (her sister's expression), which invariably ended in an argument. It grieved Crookshank that none of the paintings she'd given her only sibling were hung. There were excuses, decor and color schemes and so forth. It hurt and especially so after the small Rothko, a dark rectangle of merging maroons and blacks, appeared on the living room wall.

"It was a steal, Emmeline, an absolute steal."

Crookshank was not given to tears but she cried on the IRT local going home to Chelsea. She told Ferdinand at the front desk that her sister was a stinker. She did not really mean it. She wished they got along. They didn't have anyone else.

Miss Hooper got a dig in at least once every summer sending postcards of something thoroughly Côte d'Azur or vicinity. The latest was fields of lavender on the outskirts of Avignon. (Miss Hooper also made a yearly pilgrimage to Vence where one of her heroes, D. H. Lawrence, had died. Crookshank had received several remembrances of Lawrence's final sanatorium. She found these grim.) Max admired the lavender fields.

"They're so pretty."

"If you say so...."

It was to be expected of Miss Hooper that when she hired a cleaner it would be a dumbbell like this. Crookshank thought it a shame that you couldn't have a decent conversation with someone while they were sweeping up around you. She'd tried, God knows, but it never went anywhere.

When Westbeth had its annual flea market, Crookshank dispatched Max with specific instructions. She needed a corkscrew, a wool sweater, a brassiere, and any paints or brushes that were going cheap. (Westbeth was filled with artists who were popping off at a fair clip. Some years she got an unfinished canvas and enjoyed scraping it down.) Most importantly, Max shouldn't say for whom she was buying as that was, frankly, no one's business. It didn't help. Crookshank was accosted by one of her neighbors not long after.

"Saw your girl at the flea market buying out the place. Opening a store are we?"

That was typical of Westbeth, far off in the West Village as it was, and one reason why Crookshank missed what she called the fleshpots of Chelsea. There wasn't anyone really first rate at Westbeth, simply a pack of bourgeois time servers. (If you were first rate you wouldn't require charity. The truth must be told. Half of them were still mourning the Federal Art Project and the rest of the WPA.)

Even Miss Hooper did not engage with the other tenants, avoiding the get-togethers and pot lucks. But Miss Hooper was a Southern snob and would not know the proletariat from a circus troupe. As for Crookshank, it had to do with their lack of talent. The laurels they were living on did not come more wilted. The sweater fit but the brassiere did not. Crookshank wore the brassiere anyway. She was not finicky.

Another postcard arrived, this one of the Matisse Chapel. (Vence again, of course. Miss Hooper was Alabama Catholic and liked to pretend she was religious. Crookshank thought it was all malarkey.) A postcard like this was intended to get under the recipient's skin. Aside from hoisting a great twentieth century artist, Matisse *père*, up the flagpole at her, there was the matter of Matisse *fils*, the New York dealer. Crookshank once spent an agonizing ten minutes at Pierre Matisse's gallery in the Fuller Building as the Frenchman looked over her work with his arms folded and a lip curved like a scimitar approaching her throat.

"Hmmm," he said.

He did not say hmmm, I see. He did not say hmmm, hot dog. He did not say hmmm, whaddaya know. He said hmmm. The phone rang and Matisse seemed relieved to answer it. At that moment Crookshank knew her chance had come and gone. It was undoubtedly the best chance she would ever have. She felt foolish as if she had walked in and hollered: hey Pete, how's the old man? It was many years in the past but the horror of that day remained. She felt them still at times when she couldn't sleep.

Not long after moving to Westbeth, she and Miss Hooper were matching Gibsons and corn sticks at the Coach House. At that time it still seemed likely they might hit it off. Miss Hooper told her one: something to do with her hymen and an altar boy with buck teeth back in Mobile. Crookshank reciprocated, telling her tale of Pierre Matisse. It felt good to get it out in the open. She had kept it inside for so long. Miss Hooper laughed, spitting the onion in her Gibson onto the bar.

"That must have been so crushing for you," she said, "they say Pierre has the best eye in the business."

Crookshank had only been to Paris once, in 1956, sailing on the Île de France. The money came from a full length mink coat her mother had left. (It was not left to her but simply left; her sister didn't want it, not caring for fur.) The Ritz Thrift Store took the mink on consignment and the small windfall it produced (not exactly a Guggenheim as someone said), provided for three months in a *chambre de bonne* near Les Halles. (Crookshank was familiar with Manhattan walk-ups but six flights was a haul.)

She went round the museums and had the *plat du jour* at various small restaurants. She hoped to be taken for a *jolie laide* but feared she was a middle-aged American frump, no more chic than a mustard plaster. She walked heavily. In a mirror at the Galeries Lafayette she caught sight of a hideous pair of shoes and then recoiled when she saw her own feet were in them.

She went to see Richard Wright whom she had known well in the 1930's. She hoped for a reunion, a little laughter and tears, but Wright had fallen away from communism and the old barricades. He was grumpy, Crookshank thought, the way expatriates become. She made the mistake of praising *Giovanni's Room,* not knowing that Wright and James Baldwin were no longer speaking.

It was an awkward, almost tense, meeting that made her doubt the reality of her own youth. (Yet when Wright called her Emmeline she was pleased. She always found him a very handsome man. When his fatal heart attack came a few years later she wept.) She gained weight in France (the butter, butter everywhere and in everything) that stayed with her. Her spring overseas was not all it might have been and she was not unhappy to go home and get back to painting.

Off the coast of Nantucket, an Italian ship, the *Andrea Doria,* struck a Swedish vessel and capsized. The Île de France, returning to New York, rescued hundreds of survivors. Crookshank befriended a disheveled, shivering man, providing blankets from her cabin and cognac from her trunk. They were close in age and there was silver in his hair.

As they were docking at West 48th Street he gave her his hotel. Crookshank did not believe in fate and not in passion to be sure but as a painter she felt she must rely on the evidence of her eyes alone. She went to his hotel, it was the Savoy-Plaza, and sent up her name. The man was from Milan. He had lost his luggage and did not care to be seen in Manhattan in unsuitable clothing. Crookshank understood once again. There are only so many chances in life and when they are used up there are no more.

The night of the blackout was hot and sticky. The electricity failed about nine o'clock and with it Crookshank's two fans. She slept poorly, the oppression of humidity combining with a dread that she was not well. (There were midnight panics of blood clots, of embolisms, while she tossed and turned.) When Max arrived, it was her day, the power was back on. Max was tired. She had not had a full night's sleep for months and she had already been to Miss Bascom that morning. Crookshank sent Max back out for aspirin. She made her Yuban and turned on the radio. (She had never owned a television.)

There were reports of looting overnight, particularly in Brooklyn. One commentator drew a contrast with the previous blackout, in 1965, when a feeling of camaraderie throughout the city had prevailed. (Crookshank had a fond memory of conversation by candle light in the Chelsea lobby that evening. Her friend Moses Soyer had done shadowgraphs and Virgil

Thomson sang from one of his operas. She was fifty then, still young by all accounts.)

Max came in with the aspirin. She was short of breath from walking up the stairs. (The building's shaky elevators were being inspected.) The windows of a supermarket in Bedford-Stuyvesant had been smashed and the shelves stripped. A woman was arrested carrying out Pampers from the store.

"What the hell are those?"

Max said they were diapers. You didn't reuse them, she said. She had washed her daughter's cloth diapers in a bucket and hung them to dry on the roof. This ritual mated them the way nursing did. Having grown up on a farm she was not unused to excrement. After she had scrubbed her hands she held her daughter aloft and kissed her kneecaps. (Ah, Mr. Zwerling said, such *pulkes*.) Now she felt dizzy every morning. She did not know what would become of her daughter.

"They're a lot easier for everyone now."

"Listen to this criminality," Crookshank said. She pointed angrily at the radio. "Those people are getting out of hand."

The day was as hot as the day before. Crookshank was bothered by the noise of the vacuum cleaner. She went into her bedroom and closed the door.

Miss Hooper was home in the fall, enjoying a *jour de repos*. I am brown as a nut, she said. Crookshank was asked in for a drink (*Fais comme chez toi...*) and the Air France dinner menu was waved under her nose and both her chins.

"The *escargot en croute* was not half bad."

Crookshank was shoved into a butterfly chair from which her escape would not be easy. Miss Hooper went through her itinerary though Crookshank was not one who received a full accounting but only highlights.

"Cannes has gone quite Jewish. They come for the film festival and don't know when to leave. A pity."

The butterfly chair was being unrelievably medieval with Crookshank's backside. (They were like everything else postwar, a sham.) It was an Indian Summer day and the windows were wide. This old scarecrow comes home, Crookshank gloomed, and the weather turns glorious for her.

"I had a little fling in August. I don't mind telling you; you'll hear about it anyway." Crookshank didn't imagine she would. "It was brief but all the more glorious for that. Spend all you want on lotions, Crook, but that's the body cream that works. I feel like an ingenue after a good rubdown."

Crookshank felt like strangling her. And whoever designed this chair should be sentenced to hell. She could not move her hips an inch.

"A possibility but only just, that he may fly in this winter. He hasn't been to New York since he was...well, no details for the moment."

Keep your details but Crookshank hoped he would come. The thought of Miss Hooper prostrate at the feet of a little runt of a Mediterranean gigolo with a pencil mustache would make anyone's Christmas. She'd provide the mistletoe.

"Has this Max person been coming to you?"

"Off and on," Crookshank said, "sick or something."

"Sick? Something catching? But really, look at the state of my plants. I'll have to let her go. Frankly, I'm sorry you recommended her to me."

"I did not. I got her from you."

"That's what you say now but I'm not surprised."

Crookshank could not rise from the butterfly chair. Miss Hooper had a solution, a striped beach towel from a hotel in Nice. They each took an end and Crookshank was winched upward onto the floor.

Miss Bascom on Jane Street looked forward to Thanksgiving and having a few friends over. She asked if Max would come in that day and cook. Max had missed many days of work and could not say no. It would be very simple, Miss Bascom said. Max knew Miss Bascom was not hard to please.

On Thursday morning Max cleaned Crookshank's rooms. Crookshank was moping. Her sister had decided on Tavern on the Green for the holiday. Knowing a captain there, her sister was promised a table free of any drafts. (Warner LeRoy had done wonders with the old place and was so seductive. He'd certainly stop to say hello.) Just a small gathering this year and no cattle call as in the past. (The dining room on West End Avenue seated twelve, between a Marie Laurencin and Japanese woodblocks.) Unfortunately, there would not be room for Crookshank at the Tavern.

Max saw that she was not dressed to go out (the pedal pushers, the sweatshirt, the moccasins) and said Miss Bascom liked to have guests. Crookshank said she would consider it. At four o'clock, a little gussied up, she went to Jane Street. Max was serving the food she had prepared. Miss Bascom's usual entourage was in residence. (They did not care what they ate. They were there for the company.) Crookshank enjoyed the conversation, the anecdotes and twice-told stories. The house was not opulent but the wine was very good and the timeless old men were theatrically flirtatious.

She was interested to hear of a garden on the corner. As a homeowner on the block, Miss Bascom had a key to the gate. Crookshank longed for somewhere such as that. At eight o'clock Max told Miss Bascom she was very tired. She'd be back in the morning to clean up. Before long Crookshank was sleepy. The wine was heavy. (They were mostly Bordeaux, the last of Miss Bascom's cellar.) Crookshank said thank you and distributed business cards from her dealer. (These were gratefully accepted and quickly lost.) She put on her coat, regretful that she had never lived in a townhouse. Outside she went down the stoop carefully, her hand on the rail. Max had fallen. She was on the bottom step, her pea coat unbuttoned, her feet to the sidewalk.

"I can't move my legs," Max said.

Crookshank moved unsteadily around her. "Someone should call you a taxi."

She wanted to look at the garden. At Eighth Avenue she stopped at the fence. There was a bench inside and a birdbath and there would be morning sun. It would be, she thought, a lovely place to paint.

1992

M r. Zwerling knew his accomplishments to be few. He put a new point on his carpenter's pencil with a pen knife but there was so little to write down. Max had been gone more than ten years and that time, that era so to speak, was fruitless. There were no plans and no aspirations.

After the first stroke, the one that pulled the skin tighter across his mouth, wrenching his harelip leftward, his hopes were replaced by worry. He might go at any moment. (Like that Wonderful One-Hoss Shay, his most successful memorization in public school. His mother, who never learned English, maintained his prize certificate in her photograph album. He did not recall the poem, remembering though that the shay broke down "just as bubbles do when they burst." He supposed that was how he would go.)

Each month he cashed his Social Security check and put half of it away in the gun metal box. He did not know what else to do. He had relied too much on Mr. Feldman, which was foolish as the lawyer had known Mr. Zwerling's father and was therefore hardly young.

Mr. Feldman's cramped office on Chambers Street was shared with a city marshal and a bail bondsman. There was no receptionist or secretary. The three men faithfully answered each other's telephone, took messages, and played three-hand canasta on slow afternoons. (The city marshal had a Blimpie hero for lunch, the bail bondsman liked Chinese food, and Mr. Feldman brought something from home. When the bail bondsman had a skip and was absent, sometimes for days, the other two missed him sorely.)

Mr. Feldman mostly handled small claims, real estate closings, and some probate. He was sufficiently busy to hold his head up at the Wall Street Synagogue and had no grievance. A day came, however, when an old friend asked for help. (A man also known to Mr. Zwerling's father.) The man's grandson had been arrested for selling marijuana in Washington Square Park. The grandfather could not understand how this happened. The grandson was a good boy, a yeshiva boy, there must be a mistake.

Mr. Feldman did not enjoy criminal law. It made him anxious. The Criminal Court House on Centre Street was foreign territory and the guards there terrified him. The procedure was alien and the assistant district attorney seemed to regard him with contempt.

"She treats me like dirt under her shoe," he said to his friends at the office. They were indignant on his behalf but what can you do?

His client too was not courteous, resentful that this was the best his family would do for him. Mr. Feldman had a pacemaker. He was taking a pill at a water fountain in the Criminal

Court hallway and collapsed. He died not long after. The charge against his client was dropped when the arresting officer did not show up in court.

Mr. Zwerling's plan was to set something up with Mr. Feldman. He trusted him as his father had. He did not know who else to trust. (He feared this general mistrust would not be countenanced by a righteous God but what was to be done.)

Mr. Feldman would manage the money and see that Emmett and Salome were provided for after Mr. Zwerling was gone. It wasn't such a bad plan overall except that Mr. Feldman was no spring chicken and that was not taking into account the drug dealing putz of a grandson. (Mr. Zwerling did not regard his own bootlegging days in the same light.)

It was the stroke, of course, that left Mr. Zwerling thinking poorly. (His friend Hyman might have helped with his good head for finance but he had passed away too, indestructible as he had seemed.) There was a cloudiness, an inability to put two and two together.

He should have begun after Max died when the future became so evident. It was clear what must be arranged but Mr. Zwerling put it off as if at the same time putting off the finality of her death. Part of his difficulty was how to mourn her. He had never completely centered Max in his life. She had continued to call him Mr. Zwerling until the day she lost the power of speech. (Recently Salome had begun to call him Zayde. Where she had learned this Yiddishism was a mystery but he joyously accepted the gift of being called grandfather by Max's daughter. As he had often felt, you never knew what Salome was thinking.)

That sprig of wildness in Max never departed. It was like those paintings on the loft walls her artist friends had made. Crazy stuff, you couldn't make heads or tails of it. Where did she find them? For that matter where had she come from? He never really knew. Out west was all she ever admitted. (Out of nowhere, she liked to say.) Her birthplace was as concealed as his own thoughts about her.

Not so many generations removed from the shtetl, Mr. Zwerling accepted that everyone was entitled to a privacy of origin. There was a melting pot but it was in the middle of a busy intersection.

In old fashioned terms Max was a bit of a flapper, like the heavily mascaraed and beaded women who drank the bathtub gin he once delivered. (Terrible stuff, Mr. Zwerling recalled, but better than needled beer.) They were the good time girls though some perhaps ended up at the Sailor's Rest across the street. (That the Sailor's Rest these days had become men meeting men was not unexpected. The entire neighborhood seemed devoted to that now.)

Following his stroke Mr. Zwerling had odd recollections. There was a woman in a speakeasy who called him the cutest thing going. He was far from that but it was kind of her to say so. She kissed him on the forehead and the aroma of her loose breasts remained until it was replaced by his mother preparing stuffed cabbage. There were times now when he smelled Max near him. She was not, she would not ever be again. She wore the same perfume the many years they shared this building.

"Someone to help us bury our dead," Mr. Zwerling said. "Not to forget them but to help us bear it. That is what we hope for."

There was little going on at the store. The steady buyers were mostly departed; many of the meatpacking plants had moved elsewhere. Mr. Zwerling had a cataract he ignored. It would require a trip beyond Tenth Avenue and he no longer did that. Emmett was slower as well, often dragging his feet.

"He's lost a step."

After Max died Mr. Zwerling looked around for something for Salome to do. (Another something, yes. He should have done something about the first something then too, the money something that is. That was the important something. His father said money takes care of itself but it doesn't every time. In this instance it hasn't and there you are without anything. He should have done something, exactly, that's what he should have done, something. This failure gnawed at him. It was a muddle. It made his head spin.)

Mr. Zwerling had long donated to the Salvation Army, principally because of the shelters and their work with the alcoholic. (There was a Salvation Army collection box on the hardware store counter along with the ASPCA and the March of Dimes.) Except for very infrequent sips of slivovitz for indigestion, a habit inherited from his father, Mr. Zwerling abhorred strong drink and pitied those in thrall to it. (In this respect he regretted his bootlegging past. The slivovitz was made by a woman on Delancey Street who could have easily passed for a witch in the old country. Her age was unknown and she gave the impression of being pickled in brine.)

Mr. Zwerling inquired at the Salvation Army headquarters on 14th Street and arranged for Salome to work there. It would be a short walk and at the very least bring in a few dollars. But the important part was being occupied.

That was his concern. Salome was a young woman and should have something to keep her out of trouble. (Mr. Zwerling read the newspapers, he saw the headlines.) Things happened, terrible things, to the innocent.

"It is not a bowl of cherries out there. Not like it was."

So *nu*, one might ask, if it's not being too inquisitive, when was it ever a bowl of cherries out there? (Mr. Zwerling heard voices, echoes you might say, of those beyond the grave. His mother spoke freely to him now. She was once careful, afraid he would bear an accent in America if she kept him too close. She need not have worried. Mr. Zwerling sounded to all like precisely what he was, a New Yorker.)

Now that her mother was gone, Salome spent too much time alone. That was not good for anyone. She did not object to the job if that was what Mr. Zwerling wanted her to do. It was strange at first but she had an aptitude for routine. (Her mother on the other hand could not do the same work for very long. Like a scent behind the ear her interest began strong but soon wore off.)

Salome did not need an alarm clock and was never late. (Mr. Zwerling brought an alarm clock up from the basement that he worked on. It ran slow anyway. Salome did not bother to wind it. She kept agricultural time. It was inborn.) The first weeks he waited for her outside the store.

"How was work today?"

"It was nice. We had a fire drill."

Other than that she was up on the viaduct, rain or shine. She was up on that viaduct that had bisected his days and given his father the grief of a lifetime. (As if there was not enough grief to go around.) Now that the train no longer ran, now that it was a mile or more of useless scrap iron, Mr. Zwerling almost felt bitterness.

They told his father it was progress. (In America, his father said, that is what they call a pogrom.) All that disruption to move boxcars of dead meat. It was less than thirty years before the refrigerated trucks began to take the trade away. The carpenter's pencil scraped across the paper. It was the stroke that dumped all this in his lap. There were days when he could not get his head out of the past. Every thought ran back to its tidal dawn.

As for Salome, he hardly knew what she was up to on the viaduct with her runner beans and transition zone grasses and starter trays. Mr. Zwerling had not been on the roof for some time. He found Emmett one day raising rolls of sod onto the viaduct with a block and tackle. Mr. Zwerling so enjoyed the working of a good pulley system he forgot to ask about the sod. He walked away muttering about Archimedes.

"Now that was a thinker."

Emmett was not in agreement about the Salvation Army job for Salome. He wrote his objection down so it would be clear. Don't potchke like she is a broken percolator, he advised. Mr. Zwerling grunted. (When Emmett used Yiddish he meant business.) Well, Emmett had never appreciated the value of planning, of a blueprint. (Mr. Zwerling adored blueprints.) The trouble was, Mr. Zwerling hated to say this, Emmett was a hedonist. He was completely devoted to the pleasure principle and root beer.

"Think of the grasshopper and the ant."

Emmett never had, not being attracted to fables. One morning Mr. Zwerling was convinced he heard bleating from up there. He may have a cataract but his hearing was fine. It seems Salome had adopted a goat and Emmett came up from the basement with a baby bottle.

"But I was fed with that."

Mr. Zwerling had put the property in Emmett's name. At least Mr. Feldman had time to arrange for the transfer. It was something but it was not enough. Mr. Zwerling could not envision that this corner of Tenth Avenue would ever be worth anything. It was what the newspapers called a dubious neighborhood. (They should have been here when the ocean liners came in. Hah, they have no idea.)

And there you have it, he had not provided. He was instructed to and he had not. (He knew the Law and the Law was explicit.) He had failed in his obligations and might not live to fast on another Yom Kippur. His private atonements would not suffice. There was money in the gunmetal gray box but how long it would last them could not be foretold. That is the great divide, Mr. Zwerling thought: there are those who foretell and those who do not.

Emmett came in from the market. (He was using a bodega on Eighth Avenue now.) It was not easy getting Mr. Zwerling to eat. Neither of them was anything of a cook. They had subsisted for years on canned goods. (The solitary expeditions to Essex Street for fried goose fat were long gone like Mr. Zwerling's arteries.) Soup and crackers was their meal of choice most days. (The salt was not good for Mr. Zwerling.)

Emmett put the shopping bag on the counter. He had treats for Salome and there was her favorite, a Snickers bar. He wasn't surprised to find Mr. Zwerling with his head down. Mr. Zwerling slept poorly. His hair had been gray for many years but now it was feathery.

Emmett looked again. There was a blotch on Mr. Zwerling's neck below the ear. It sometimes happened that Emmett opened his mouth as if to speak. It meant the directions his mind gave him were in conflict. He put his hand on Mr. Zwerling's shoulder. There was no need to shake him. Emmett looked out at Tenth Avenue. They had put a bell on the front door but it did not ring. There were empty shelves and at the moment (he'd realized this that morning) they did not have a broom to sell. He meant to make a note about it but had forgotten. When old Mr. Zwerling brought him here the first time he was frightened. There were people going in and out but then he saw the train running above and he put his hands together and clapped.

Mr. Zwerling was a lifelong member and contributor to the Hebrew Free Burial Association, as his father had been. It provided kaddish services for his parents. To an extent this was mumbo jumbo, Mr. Zwerling judged, but mumbo jumbo has its uses. Most importantly, the association buried the indigent.

"God protect the poor Jew."

Mr. Zwerling left instructions in the gunmetal gray box. There was a telephone number. He was not indigent but had arranged for the association to see about his funeral.

"Don't want to be a bother."

Emmett waited for Salome to come home. (In this instance it was easier to show than to tell. She had seen her mother die but this was peaceful, more like the creatures she raised on the viaduct. They went quietly too.) There was a call to make and Emmett could not do it. She was agitated at using the heavy rotary telephone. (Mr. Zwerling had declined the pushbutton plastic replacements, due to his great fondness for bakelite.) The dial was difficult to use and Salome held her breath with each turn. A man answered.

"Mr. Zwerling is dead."

Salome gripped the receiver with two hands. She was afraid she had said the wrong thing or said it too fast. She had wanted to say Zayde but didn't know if she was allowed to.

"I understand. I will come right away."

The next day a car took Emmett and Salome to Staten Island. She had never seen so many trees. Staten Island was the other side of the Statue of Liberty. Max showed it to her when they walked along the piers. At the grave there were men praying. She was happy her grandfather had so many friends. The car brought them back to Tenth Avenue. Salome went up to the loft. She had things to do on the viaduct but sat for a while looking through her mother's scrapbooks. Emmett did not open the store. He disconnected the telephone and went to his room and closed the door. There was a small mirror above his dresser. He covered it with a towel and sat in his chair by the window.

1958

Because Jenny Diver was leaving the cast, libations were planned at Chumley's for after the show. (There were rumors of a part in *Flower Drum Song* but Jenny was not saying. She had television credits too so anything was possible.)

Everyone was going except the Streetsinger who said he had a previous engagement. He was instructed to "bring her along " but it was more a matter of bringing him along and the Streetsinger was not ready for that. Otherwise it would be the usual crowd for Jenny Diver was popular and a good sport. (There had been two other Jenny Divers between her and Lotte Lenya at the beginning and she was the best except for Lotte.)

The new one coming in was unknown and Macheath told Mr. Peachum *sotto voce* he'd heard she put it out there to get the role and there you have it. Mr. Peachum raised an eyebrow at that but not very high. He'd been banging around the theater since the Barrymores and was not surprised at much. Pray God she can sing was all he said.)

They called ahead to Chumley's to arrange some tables together. All were looking forward to a few drinks unfettered

by out-of-towners as that was, after three years, their princi-
pal audience for *The Threepenny Opera*. It wasn't easy to find
Chumley's if you weren't told how and they, you could be very
sure, were not telling.

Max had the front rows, putting the seat cushions up, checking for anything that would give the vacuum cleaner indigestion. There could be apple cores, banana peels, Chiclet boxes,
handkerchiefs, sometimes a corn muffin or a hatpin. Francine
said it was very Elizabethan but it seemed to Max just messy.
(Fortunately it was a good show and nothing was thrown at the
performers.)

Francine was a drama student. Not the acting kind but someone who reads plays and wants to write about them. She could
really go on about Ben Jonson and Thomas Massinger if you
weren't careful and what she didn't know about Shakespeare
probably was not worth knowing. She was not, though, to any
degree, stage struck. Nothing ruined good blank verse like some
knucklehead from Yonkers in doublet and hose on his high
horse. Seriously, she said, they all make a mess of it.

"Ask Christopher Marlowe if you don't believe me."

The vacuum cleaner did not object to grapes, raisins, loose
Milk Duds, or pocket change. Aside from concern about the
vacuum's digestive tract, dropped coins gave their post-perfor-
mance cleaning some spice. Max used a flashlight but Francine
(self-described as part aardvark) could spot a nickel or subway
token six seats over.

"Where but by chance a silver drop hath fallen."

That was for a dime. They pooled their gleanings and could come away with a dollar or dollar fifty each some nights. Matinees for some reason were not as lucrative. Max had been ushering at the Theatre de Lys since September, working weekends. Francine, who had a telephone, filled in when needed. Their spelunking (a word Max learned from Francine, something to do with caves) was more fun when they did it together. The night watchman was very protective of his Hamilton-Beach upright and despaired of the day when it might gobble up a fatal bottlecap.

"Thoughts high for one so tender, cleft the heart."

Francine was not attending the party as her boyfriend (whom she called "my benedict") did not approve of her "mingling." As for Francine, she felt mingling was what she needed. She and her benedict were saving themselves for marriage and it was getting to her in the worst way possible.

"And so the general of hot desire was sleeping by a virgin hand disarm'd."

It was frustrating, having a monkey on her back. (Francine had been to a run-through of a new Living Theatre production about drug addiction.)

"I dug the lingo," she said, "natch."

She'd read somewhere that "you-know-what" was good for acne. (A medical fact, she thought, or they wouldn't say so.) Francine was a trifle splotchy in general and once a month ("like clockwork") out they came. Max couldn't say. She'd never had a pimple in her life and though there were a few wrinkles around her eyes her skin was as clear as it had ever been.

Francine had been applying Ice-O-Derm for two months and was taking yeast supplements but so far her complexion, as she called it, had not improved. Recently she'd seen something about nymphomania in *Sexology*. (Monthly at the newsstand, 35 cents, she read it standing up until they yelled at her.) She wondered if nymphomaniacs felt the way she did. She felt a little, well, pent up in the morning and pent up at night.

Looking through *Cue* magazine (she bought that) for a foreign movie she saw an ad for Mateus Rosé. Just the thing. an artistic film and some Mateus might just be what the doctor ordered. Her benedict didn't think so. He said they should save the wine for a special occasion and stay home to watch *Gunsmoke* with his parents.

That was disappointing. Three quarters left on a seat, however, cheered her up. She was saving for her benedict's Christmas present (an electric shaver, he had acne too) and maybe some fine sandpaper for the two of them. Max had her eye on some Keds for her daughter. Salome needed them. Keeping up with her mother on the street was not easy at her age and sneakers would help.

They heard the night watchman revving up his Hamilton-Beach. Once his work was done he set out his portable television set in the lobby to watch *The Late Show* and then *The Late, Late Show*. He had a German accent and the TV had rabbit ears. Francine and Max collected discarded programs and saved any that could be used again. (Visitors took them home. New Yorkers threw them in the aisle.)

They put on their coats and the night watchman let them out onto Christopher Street. Francine would have liked to kiss Max goodbye but her acne made her shy. They had such a good time working together. It wasn't everybody you could talk to about that intimate stuff and she could talk to Max. Francine sighed:

"Your daughter and the Moor are now making the beast with two backs. Oh that lucky Desdemona. Adieu..."

Max went quickly down Bedford Street, thinking about kindergarten and Keds. If she got Keds a size larger they might last a year. Salome could wear two pairs of socks until she grew into them. Max went past the front of Chumley's to the side entrance around the corner on Barrow. It was down an alleyway. This was left over from Prohibition, she was told, when the bar was a speakeasy. It was the cognoscenti way to go in and Mr. Zwerling knew it well.

"That was a hot spot."

Mr. Zwerling was amused that Max was an usher (or usherette as he put it.) He'd considered it too at one time. A portion of his childhood bootlegging profits were spent on Broadway revues where he developed hopeless infatuations on showgirls. If he became an usher he could see them for free.

"That's over the hill and far away."

Max came in the back room. It was smoky and smelled of hamburger and cigarettes. She slipped between two men playing darts to the *Threepenny* tables. When Macheath saw Max he jumped up and got her a Bass ale at the bar. She did not care for beer nowadays but it gave Macheath a chance to sing.

"Bass's ale by the pail, he would order Rosanna to go out and buy..."

Macheath could be show-offy but he was the lead. Max squeezed in between Polly Peachum and Lucy Brown. There were peanuts and beer nuts on the table and what looked like the remains of a club sandwich, some toothpicks and a pickle slice. Max had not eaten since the morning and began picking at peanuts. This was the second time she'd been out with the cast and it was a treat to be with them with their greasepaint off. They were different in their street clothes. In the theater they often seemed to be not fully genuine. Jenny Diver was laughing very loudly and the faces of the others were inquiring.

They were trying to get her drunk enough to tell them what she had lined up. *Threepenny* was steady employment. You rarely left the company unless you'd found something better. Lucy was particularly interested because she and Jenny were the same age and shared the same agent. (Lucy had done a toothpaste commercial and though only her mouth was shown she was still being paid for it. A man on the subway, Woodlawn line, said he'd know her mouth anywhere and she hit him with her pocketbook. And he had bad teeth, she said.)

It was apparently up to Macheath to wheedle it out of Jenny. "So what is it, a movie maybe?"

Jenny pretended she didn't hear. Macheath drummed two fingers on his upper lip. He wasn't giving up that easily. They laughed about the Streetsinger who gave women's names to the men he saw.

"Really, can't he think of anything better than that?"

The Streetsinger was sure it was an excellent subterfuge but it did not fool anyone except Suky Tawdry. She thought the Streetsinger was nothing short of divine. Verging on Rock Hudson she sighed.

"So Antonia for Anthony..."

"And Georgina for George."

Suky did not accept it. She implied they were only saying this because the Streetsinger was so handsome.

"Go home and have your mother explain it to you."

"But not too much detail please."

"You're all jealous because he has such..."

Suki could not think of the word. She was on her third rye and ginger ale and near the halls of melancholy. Mr. Peachum hoped he would be allowed to escort her back to her apartment (shared with another actress, currently resting, and two hamsters) and to that end was encouraging her to use a straw.

"One too few, my dear, can be as calamitous as one too many."

Another round came and Macheath was on his feet again. *"Dublin stout, he would shout, keep drinking and never say die..."*

The word came to Suki with a hiccup. "He has presence."

She meant the Streetsinger. He did have presence, a fact acknowledged by all. Whatever it is separating the walk-on from the matinee idol, that presence was there in him, that mysterious alchemy. (When the Streetsinger joined the ensemble Macheath put lifts in his shoes, the only noticeable change being vertigo.)

The Streetsinger opened the show with "Mack the Knife" and for the others it was a matter of catching up. If there was a casting director in the audience their eyes, like those of everyone else, could not be drawn away from the Streetsinger.

"Well, there's always *Sergeant Preston of the Yukon.*"

This was a reference to Polly Peachum who had done an episode of *Sergeant Preston* where she was plunged in a freezing river and chased by a grizzly.

"Exit, pursued by a bear."

"Is it true the huskies had fleas?"

"Oh but there were roses in your cheeks."

Jenny Diver had her chin in the palm of her hand. She would miss all this. You never knew how a new show would work out or how you would be received. Macheath was a ham and Mr. Peachum was a flirt and Lucy Brown borrowed money and Polly had her terrible Joan Crawford impersonation and that was all just fine. It was just fine.

"Hooray for Hollywood?"

"Give my regards to Broadway?"

"The new Channel 11 weather girl? I knew it. What's the forecast? Should we bring our umbrellas tomorrow?"

Jenny Diver maintained a straight face. She supposed she should say something but it seemed so nervy and almost unfair. All day she tried to think of something casual and off-hand. Again and again she'd thought of the same line.

"Well, ya'll, I'll be practicing my Southern accent y'know."

Macheath looked at Mr. Peachum and Suki Tawdry looked at Lucy Brown. They all looked at one another and then at Jenny Diver. Max too felt the excitement as the two words began to form in the actor's minds.

"Tennessee Williams."

Their cheering was heard throughout the bar. They were congratulating Jenny Diver when the waiter brought more drinks. Someone in the other room had paid for a round but was requesting a song.

"I think we can manage that."

"You mean you think you can manage that."

Macheath refused to take offense. He jetted around the table, grandly beckoning with his hands. He pulled Max to her feet, singing over her head, holding her tightly. They danced through the sawdust as drinkers raised their glasses and shouted encouragement. It was grand to be alive.

Oh the shark has pretty teeth, dear...

Out of character, Jenny Diver began to cry.

1980

The hospital supply warehouse on Houston Street was busy. It was wholesale but Mr. Zwerling knew the owner. They went way back and Hyman liked to talk about the days when they "ran liquor" as if they'd been anything more than a couple of snots picking up loose change under the El.

Even so, Hyman was a big *macher* now with one son who was already way up at Sloan-Kettering and another the same at Maimonides. His father had been a cantor and a high muckety-muck in his own right. It ran in the family like dimples.

Hyman had long had a connection at the Municipal Building when it came to purchase orders for city institutions and then, more recently, a second golden goose appeared in the form of nursing homes, a growing industry. Hyman liked to say he was slipping a bedpan under every Jewish *tuches* that didn't get shipped down to Florida. Success had carried him out to four thousand square feet in Great Neck. (Where, he confessed, they were "rattling around.")

This was good for Mr. Zwerling who no longer had to make excuses about attending Hyman's family seders at his apartment in Peter Cooper Village. Mr. Zwerling liked a seder, the talk and the ritual, the longer the better, it brought his mother and father to mind and reminded him who he was.

Yet he felt like a poor relation at Hyman's table, a childless bachelor with a failing business. After some years he contrived not to go any longer. Mr. Zwerling did not mean to complain. Hyman had been good to him. It was just that he made you know it. Hyman had been to Israel several times and of this Mr. Zwerling, a man not prone to envy, was envious. As soon as you get off the plane, Hyman told him, your heart bursts with pride.

"Bubbeleh, what can I do you?"

Hyman was on the phone. Hyman was always on the phone. Mr. Zwerling's telephone had not rung all week. He said he needed a wheelchair.

"You don't look it, mayn chaver."

Mr. Zwerling felt it. His first Social Security check had arrived the previous month. The money was welcome but the implication was not. It was the implications, God knows, that puts the second foot in the grave. The wheelchair was for a neighbor, he said.

"You brought Emmett?"

If Hyman coveted anything from Mr. Zwerling, it was Emmett. That *schwartze* was a gift, a magician with his hands. Hyman had once tried to hire Emmett away and was puzzled by the negative reaction. Still you could not argue with that kind of thing. Hyman was married to a woman most generously described as a harridan or possibly a *mekhasheyfe*. She had driven their sons to succeed and hosannas were raised when they left Peter Cooper Village. Hyman was devoted to her. There was family and work, there was nothing else. Mr. Zwerling said Emmett was busy.

"I'll send it with the truck."

Mr. Zwerling said he would walk it up, to get the feel of it. That Social Security check did not mean he was a corpse yet. Hyman made a face but a gentle one. This was how his old friend had been since forever. Instead of looking after the store he was taking a leisurely stroll up Tenth Avenue with a wheelchair, his head in the clouds. It was not as if he had children to look after him. (Yes, no doubt about it, he'd let that *punim* of his hold him back.) Mr. Zwerling knew that face. Hyman would be mentioning Sophie any second.

"If you'd followed my advice and told Sophie..."

Leave it to Hyman to be again going on about a girl they went to the World's Fair with. And not the recent World's Fair. This is the 1939 World's Fair we're talking about. He might as well be quoting from the Talmud. Sophie was a nice girl, plump, peaches and cream. A few of them went around together. Mr. Zwerling could never bring himself to ask her out on his own. And then the war came and she married a soldier at the last minute.

A workman brought a wheelchair out and unfolded it. Hyman dropped a small box of hamantaschen on the seat.

"Happy Purim. They're from Kossar's so save some for Emmett."

On the way home Mr. Zwerling stopped at the Square Meal for coffee. (He did not like the Swee-Touch-Nee tea bags the Square

Meal used.) It was never as crowded as it once was. Taxi drivers came in and left just as quickly. It was the meat packers who used to crowd the place but there were fewer of them these days.

Mr. Zwerling took his coffee to go, nibbling a hamantaschen. Now, thanks to Hyman, he had Sophie on the brain. She was like a dumpling and he put his arm around her when they rode in the Futurama at the Fair. She was a great reader, indeed she was. She told him about a man who dipped a cookie in his tea and remembered his past life. That's right, it happens, that's how the mind works. Mr. Zwerling had not been to Kossar's for many years. Grand Street was not so far yet he never seemed to leave his corner anymore. There was still a lot to see if you kept your eyes open.

"She knew him for two weeks and they went to City Hall. What can you do? The war did that a lot."

Mr. Zwerling put the wheelchair in the store, leaving the Closed sign facing out. He went up to the loft. He wished there was something he could fix but there was nothing there to fix. He could not fix her, he could not help. There was nothing he could do. He was a useless old man, weak and tiresome, a *schmegegge* like you wouldn't believe. On the one hand (one hand, not even two, mind you) he counted the people who had most touched his heart and there was nothing he could fix, nothing he could do, hopeless dreamer that he was.

These days Salome maintained the loft as well as her mother had. Max's paintings were not holding up well. The changes in temperature he supposed. The big one on the wall with all the pinks and yellows was flaking. How many years ago now since he first saw them? Max had laughed a bit at his incomprehension but he did not pry. That was a part of her life he did not understand. It had come and gone, he supposed, like other things in her world.

Mr. Zwerling sighed and heard the Silvercup van drive in. Emmett would carry Max up the stairs. Mr. Zwerling did not like to witness this and went down to his floor to wait. He made tea and looked at the newspaper. They put things in the *Post* nowadays you could not imagine. He heard Emmett's heavy feet on the outside staircase and the door to the loft open and close. He waited. He used to hear Max come home late. She would tap lightly on his door and say goodnight, Mr. Zwerling, goodnight. He did not drink his tea. It had no taste. The Square Meal coffee was bitter in his throat.

"Might as well hear what's what."

Salome was downstairs beside the wheelchair when Mr. Zwerling walked in. She had a blue sticker on her coat that said Visitor. St. Vincent's had released her mother after some tests. There had been tests before that. Salome went to the counter. She picked up the carpenter's pencil and wrote on a pad. She wrote laboriously. (That was a problem in school.) She wrote a name phonetically and showed it to Mr. Zwerling. All the way from the hospital she tried hard to hold the name in her head.

"Who's that?"

It came to Mr. Zwerling when he said it aloud. "Lou Gehrig."

Salome asked again who that was. Mr. Zwerling, having just stopped thinking of Sophie, went back in time again. "He was a baseball player, Sal. A very great player for the Yankees. Born right here in Manhattan. A good man and very respectful. My father hoped he was Jewish but I don't think so. But we had Hank Greenberg."

"He was sick?"

"Hank Greenberg? No..."

"This man." Her fingers were on the writing pad.

Mr. Zwerling dropped his hands to his sides. "Yes, yes, Lou Gehrig, a terrible thing, a very cruel thing. That disease is famous from him. He was in the prime of life, the prime of life. They called him the Iron Horse, Sally, because he was so strong."

"That's what momma has. They said that. I heard them."

Mr. Zwerling put two fingers to his forehead. "Oh," he said, "I see." He thought without meaning to of when he first saw her. She was living with that cuckoo painter right after the war, on Weehawken Street. Maybe she reminded him of Sophie, a little zaftig like a juicy plum. Mr. Zwerling put his hand on Salome's head. She had hair like Emmett but it was soft. Emmett was grizzled but he was old too. The two men had grown old together, a mitzvah, not one you would have reckoned. (The thought occurred: My God, we're like the Collyer brothers.)

Mr. Zwerling held Salome's hand. They went up to the loft, Mr. Zwerling carrying the box of hamantaschen.

It was longest when it was dark. Max waited for the skylight to brighten. The last train had gone by the year before or perhaps the year before that. (She could not say, she lost track of things easily.) She missed that noise. It might have been something to anticipate, something to break the day into segments that could be more easily managed. Depending on how she was positioned (as Salome turned her every few hours) Max watched the development of the Pollock or the Dutch Boy de Kooning out of the shadows. In the evening she saw them shuttered again like the slow closing of a curtain.

When Max could still sit up on her own, when she could still speak a little, Mr. Zwerling knocked on the door. A woman had stopped in the hardware store asking about the loft. She'd come in a taxi and told the driver to wait. The woman worked for *ARTnews* and had heard a rumor, on two occasions actually, of privately held paintings over in the old meatpacking district. When she came in Max smelled Chanel and liked the woolen wrap dress the woman wore. (Like her mind, Max's eyes were furiously active. She closed them to rest. She could not shut her mind.)

One of the last trains ran that afternoon and the woman was startled by its approach and the shaking of the floor. She looked at the walls, at the Pollock and the Motherwell and the de Koonings. (The door to the toilet was open with towels draped over it. She went past it, missing that de Kooning panel, the one that had frightened Salome in childhood. She missed the Franz Kline too.) She'd brought a camera but did not take it out of her shoulder bag. There was no reason to remember them.

They were interesting copies but they were nothing more than that obviously. (A graduate, no doubt, of the Paint By Numbers school.) The woman in the chair, hardly upright with a trickle of saliva at the corner of her mouth, appeared to be drunk, if not a little cracked in the head. Max could not get her words out. She sputtered when she tried too hard. Each painting had a little story that went with it.

Another time she could have offered the woman coffee, a little Sambuca, they might have talked all afternoon. If she could explain, the woman in the wrap dress would understand. Max was afraid of what she thought, that they weren't real. That was like saying something worse. The woman smiled politely. She did not like wild goose chases. She left and went downstairs. Her taxi's engine was running.

Max listened to WNYC many hours of the day. The familiar voices were like people coming to visit. She knew when to expect them and when they would leave. Once in a while you learned things about them: where they were from and where they lived now. (There was a man's voice one morning. She thought he was from Indiana but she could not be sure and he did not say.)

They went on vacations and sometimes were not there. Then she missed them. They were informative. They told you it was Easter or the Fourth of July. She liked to hear about Halloween. (They had never gone trick or treating, it was not the neighborhood for that.) There were jazz musicians who passed away. Lenny Tristano died and then Mingus. When Mingus died they played "Goodbye Pork Pie Hat" but Max could not turn her head to hear better.

There were reviews of books and restaurants. There were women who went all over the world, to curious places, to dangerous places, telling a story. She wondered if they had children and who took care of them. She heard words she did not know, foreign expressions, the name of a river. There seemed to be more countries than ever before. There was no way to find out more. She could only ask herself and she did not know the answers. When she came to New York she meant to do so much but hadn't. She had not learned anything.

When Salome went up to the roof and onto the viaduct she took the alarm clock with her. They had never used it to wake up and often forgot to wind it. She set it for two hour intervals so she did not stay outside too long. She liked a morning walk along the tracks and one in the evening. (Sunrise and sunset had always ruled them, madonna and child.) When she came down she turned her mother on the bed and rubbed her hands and feet for ten minutes. She changed her.

Salome had been given a printed sheet of instructions. (Max was given instructions too when Salome was born.) Mr. Zwerling explained what Salome did not at first understand. She was better at it now but she looked through the instructions every day to ensure she was not missing anything.

In school they often said she had missed something, that she was not paying attention as she should. She understood that her mother, most of all, wanted her to talk. She was sorry she could not talk like Clarkie. This was a nurse at St. Vincent's, who came on her own after her shift to see Max.

Clarkie had a musical voice and filled the air with conversation. She brought supplements that could be drunk through a straw and chatted and chatted. On her first visit Clarkie carried a comfort cross in her purse. (She had a box of them at home on Edgecombe Avenue.) They were made of olive wood and came from the Holy Land. (Said to be from the Garden of Gethsemane. This was not assured but Clarkie preferred to think so.)

The cross, hand carved, could be held snugly in the palm of a hand and brought such peace and solace as needed. When Clarkie saw the paintings she discreetly left the cross on the nightstand. (Recognizing it as an old icebox. Her sister in Barbados still used one.) She accepted that Jesus, as is His intent, was already present in spirit. (Clarkie liked the Jackson Pollock and was moved to see cigarette butts embedded in it. That's what it means to be carried away. She was not a smoker herself but knew of rapture.) The second time Clarkie came she washed Max's hair and cut it. She held a pocket mirror up to Max as a sunbeam fell through the skylight.

The spasms had lessened but then came back. Salome came down the ladder to find her mother on the floor. (Max weighed considerably less than she had and Salome could pick her up.) There were convulsions that frightened her. In time the spasms passed once again and Max slept more. In the spring it was Salome's habit to ask her mother if he wanted to go out. As with most questions if Max closed her eyes it meant no.

One morning Max's eyes did not shut. She blinked their sign for yes. Emmett came up when he was called. He carried Max downstairs. The wheelchair was in the store. (Emmett had kept the wheels pumped up.) Emmett and Mr. Zwerling watched from the window as Salome paused, trying to cross Tenth Avenue to the piers. She thought they would sit in the sun but then felt her mother's body resisting. (It was nearly like pressure or a quickening.)

Salome began to push them south on West Street, downtown, and Max's body relaxed. The wheelchair shuddered on the Belgian blocks and there were robins in the traffic median. At Tenth Street Max tried to slide to the left. Salome felt it and turned the wheelchair onto the sidewalk. They went a half-block and she again felt her mother's tension. It was Weehawken Street. Salome had never seen it before. Two men were unloading sheetrock from a truck. Another man in painter's whites was climbing a ladder. Salome went forward until Max made a sound. It meant stop. There was a barn door beside them. Max struggled to be closer to it and Salome lifted her hand until her mother's fingers reached the door. They kept them there. It seemed to be enough for Max.

1996

Salome was on the viaduct, in her red cotton bandana, mulching and turning soil. She'd discovered unusual scat on the tracks and breaking it apart found seeds she didn't recognize and what might be the stem of an unknown feather. She often thought of predators, newcomers both thrilling and frightening. It was sad to lose chickens but wolves and coyotes had to live too. She supposed any hunters would smell her before she smelled them.

She'd taken to defecating on the viaduct. The loft toilet was cracked. It leaked and she'd shut the water off. Emmett was too weak to replace a toilet bowl and was now often mystified by repairs he could no longer make. (He looked at tools as if baffled by what to do with them, sometimes wondering to whom they belonged.)

Now that it was warmer Salome was sleeping beside the tracks again. She liked to be near everyone and to see the moon above her head. Her mother had stitched her name onto the sleeping bag. (Salome remembered hearing they did that for camp. There was a place called Bear Mountain where children went and spent the summer. They made bracelets from gum wrappers and had bonfires.)

Earlier in the week the weather changed suddenly and a light snow fell. She was awoken by snowflakes melting on her cheek. She pulled a tarp over her to keep the sleeping bag dry and remained cocooned with the others until the sun rose. By eight o'clock it was brighter. The snow had burned off and Salome dressed and went to work.

Salome had begun menopause. Her mother had explained it to her, believing it came early in their family. (As did the first bleeding part. Max's mother said to Max: good luck to you now, missy.) Salome heard a woman at the Salvation Army speaking of menopause. This was in the ladies's room. It was mostly whispers and she did not hear clearly. She would have liked to hear more.

Salome gained weight and sometimes began to cry when there was no reason for it. At work Lorraine from Queens (from the far reaches, as she put it, to emphasize the length of her journey) monitored the morning and afternoon coffee breaks.

"It is my domain," she pronounced.

She stood by the coffee urn, a little vigilant, watching the sugar and the creamer. Salome had hoped to help someday, to tidy up beside Lorraine and leave it all ready for the next time. (There was never a happier day than when she learned to make the coffee she brought to her mother in bed. Max sometimes had cinnamon sticks that she gave Salome after stirring her coffee.)

One morning there was a meeting on their floor and more staff than usual crowded the coffee station. Lorraine was a bit overwhelmed. (She was not at her best when hurried.) Salome came up beside her to replace the paper napkins from a box. Her arm nudged the styrofoam cup holding coffee stirrers. The stirrers fell to the floor like pick up sticks as Lorraine herself spilled a plate of Pepperidge Farm cookies. She was exasperated.

"Now look what you've done, you stupid child."

Salome went to the ladies's room. She stood at the sink, her chest heaving painfully. Her eyes were very red and she washed her face twice before going back outside. After that she remained at her desk during the coffee breaks. (Salome's metal desk was delivered by a company that had employed her mother years before. The owner was the only man who ever gave Max perfume.)

There was less for Salome to do than there had been. Once there were other girls who did what she did but one by one they were taken away. (That meeting where Lorraine became so upset was called to address the shortage of simple laboring jobs. Fewer dishwashers were needed, fewer messengers and ditch diggers. The vagrant men waited on benches in the hall. They weren't allowed to smoke there any longer. There was work clearing lead paint and asbestos from public school buildings. The elderly were recommended as they would die before the asbestos could kill them and lead paint affects only children. In the first grade Salome had nibbled paint chips she peeled from the walls. She wasn't hungry. It was a craving.)

There were days Salome had nothing to do at the Salvation Army. She sat with her hands folded or looked through the drawers of her desk. The drawers were empty.

On the viaduct, Salome used a hammer and chisel on the osprey stand. (The dried bird dung was like mortar but the work was rewarding.) She sensed in the wind, in the approaching warmth, their arrival from their southern grounds. Once the ospreys lighted it had become Salome's practice to stay off the viaduct for two days as the birds began their housekeeping. (How many eggs would there be this year? She felt the anticipation like a gentle shiver down her spine.)

Once they were settled she appeared softly on the roof and walked over the middle staging plank to the tracks. (A wing might be raised but then settled back.) It was hard to stay away from her garden but this was a new generation who must come to know her. She still called them George and Martha, names she remembered from her mother reading aloud. She cherished their intelligent eyes and parental instinct and though she had no inkling of romance she believed they loved one another. (She wondered if their wings ever touched on their long flights.)

"I am here, my darling, I am here beside you."

These birds heralded the onset of abundance and Salome's months aboveground. Behind her, her new tortoise emerged from under the pomegranate bush. Emmett had found it in a vacant lot on one of his walks. (She did not know the location. Emmett seemed to travel further each time, as if trying to return somewhere.) The tortoise was a man-about-town, interested in everything. (He turned up in her sleeping bag and she waved an admonitory forefinger at him. Bad turtle, she said.)

When June came there would be further ripening and her roses would bloom. Salome liked heat, directly from the sky. That winter Emmett had trouble running the furnace. There were days when it was very cold in the loft but even winter sunshine, crisping the tar paper, raised her temperature. She sat by the trapdoor, waiting, expecting, as her eternal viaduct came back to life.

Cleaning the osprey stand left Salome thirsty. Emmett, she hoped, might have root beer. Downstairs she sniffed the metallic penetrating odor of burnt aluminum. He had left a pan on the stove, again, boiling away until the water was gone. The door between his room and the store was open but he was not there. There was clothing strewn about, the work clothes he perpetually wore. (There was a gandy dancer on the tracks who hailed Emmett now and again. The man once tossed a pair of striped railroad trousers onto the roof. Emmett wore them humbly until they were ragged.)

Salome cleaned up after Emmett. He soiled himself. (His forgetfulness was a scold, like the punishment in a Greek myth.) After Mr. Zwerling's death he continued to sell old stock but in the last year he had ceased opening the store. He rearranged the shelves and rummaged in the basement as Mr. Zwerling had. He was troubled, upset by failures he could not express. He studied the documentation Mr. Zwerling had left, pounding his fists on the counter. Aware of his anger he went out, walking to the point of exhaustion.

On the street Emmett had tremors of fearfulness and felt he must at all costs avoid the police. (They were undoubtedly looking for him. What had he done? He did not remember and could not speak in his own defense.) He sometimes mistook other uniforms for policemen and waited in building alcoves or crouched behind cars until they passed. He'd put water on for tea but then heard a siren. It was not a fire truck. He knew that sound, this was the law, the hammer. They were on Tenth Avenue.

Emmett went out the side door with the thought of hiding in the Silvercup van. He stopped. That's where they would look first. It was too late to climb up to the viaduct. He stumbled out to the street and east, past the abandoned meatpacking plants. He'd forgotten his shoes and ran in his stocking feet. He'd come out in his work pants and a pajama top. The air was cold and his breathing painful. Another patrol car passed him on Eighth Avenue and he waited beside a fire hydrant, inhaling through his mouth.

He was afraid to look back, not wanting to turn his head. At Seventh Avenue he collided with the delivery bike of a Chinese restaurant. The delivery man fell into the street. Emmett stumbled over him into the intersection. A meter maid at the southeast corner stepped off the sidewalk, moving quickly. Emmett threw up his arms. It was beginning to rain. The M20 bus coming south hit Emmett, the elongated rear view mirror knocking him over. The bus braked. The driver opened her door and stood over him. She began to scream. The meter maid got on her radio. When the ambulance arrived Emmett was dead. There was no blood. He was taken to the Bellevue morgue and held for thirty days. After that, there being no way to identify him, he was buried on Hart's Island by prisoners.

Salome left her scythe with Emmett to sharpen. He hadn't. She took it back to the viaduct. The milkweed was looking better and the Indian paintbrush. There'd been a blight that puzzled her but she'd experimented with baking soda and it seemed to help. She loved butterflies more than most things. There was rain coming. She turned her face upward to it. There was a sound. Closing her eyes, the scythe at her side, she held her breath, tucking two fingers under her bandana. It might be them.

She did not mean to be impatient. Salome opened her eyes and looked west over the river. The wings were so distant, she couldn't be sure. It was fully raining. She went quickly across the staging plank and down to the loft. The rain was prominent on the roof. If it was the osprey coming they should have a clear field. She was sorry to be stuck at home but it was exciting too. When she felt this way it was hard to know what to do. That morning she'd been looking at her mother's matchbooks. They were on the floor beside the splattered coffee can Max had kept them in. None of them had matches missing; her mother preserved them intact. (Salome bought a pack of Marlboros that she kept open on the icebox nightstand. There was an ashtray, from Schrafft's, and a lighter without fluid.)

Salome liked the matchbook colors and the restaurant names: PETER'S BACKYARD, LUCHOW'S, JUMBLE SHOP, CHEZ VOUS, MINETTA TAVERN, LYCHEE TREE. The addresses were there. She had a plan to visit them someday. (A Sunday like today would be best. If she started early the sidewalks would not be busy. No one would notice her standing there or call her names.)

MARY'S, the FIVE SPOT, the HALF NOTE, O. HENRY'S. On the inside of the matchbooks Max had written dates and sometimes a note: Frank Reading, My Birthday, After the Vernissage, Bill Evans, Margaret's Wedding. Salome put the matchbooks in rows. THE PEPPER POT, NANCY'S, EL FARO. It was such fun, like a game. THE VILLAGE BARN. That was the square dancing her mother told her about. Max had been good at that and they danced in the loft, their hands meeting and retreating.

"I'm here, my darling, here beside you."

Her mother had been to so many places. It was cold on the floor. A door slammed downstairs. She hoped that Emmett had come back, out of the rain. More than once he'd come home drenched and shivering. She looked. It wasn't Emmett, it was the wind.

1939

M ax's uncle stopped, waited, and went into the house. His left leg dragged but there was nothing wrong with it. There were days when he was like that. This time it meant he'd been to the bank where they looked at his boots to see how much mud, how much chickenshit was on them. There was some, usually. The bank had pictures of Lincoln and William Henry Harrison on the wall. Above them was Roosevelt. Another farmer, also waiting but in a better suit, said he did not know if he would vote for the president again. Seems funny, he said, another term, a third term.

"Best sight I ever saw was when they took old man Hoover down."

The man desired to spit but the bank did not have spittoons any longer. His suit was better but there was a good sized moth-hole in one shoulder. He had a buff colored envelope with his papers in it. Max's uncle had a plain white one. He knew Lincoln hadn't liked farming and he was a great man. Max's uncle took some satisfaction in that.

He had satisfaction in little else. He remembered the day the bank almost went under. There was eighty dollars in his account and he stood with the crowd on the sidewalk watching for the doors to open. One of the tellers inside fainted from fright. He had eighty dollars in the world and he was scaring an old woman because he was scared too. When the doors didn't open he went home. When the doors didn't open they weren't bank depositors; they were a mob and he never wanted any part of that. As it was the bank didn't fail but the eighty dollars was long gone nonetheless.

He'd walked to town but got a ride back with the mail carrier. So he was home sooner. Max was in the kitchen. She'd made corn bread with molasses. She supposed the next time she looked the skillet would be missing too. When you had land, sun, and rain you had everything you needed. You were told that and yet it wasn't true. Land, sun, and rain left out many things the way the Ten Commandments did.

Her uncle did not believe in naming animals. He never had so many that it mattered. He had sold two cows and possibly he was cheated. Her uncle had a nature that brought out larceny in the most honest temperament.

She did not blame him as her mother had not blamed him for his special brand of incompetence. That was at the root of everything. You could call it hard luck but hard luck as well as good luck requires a starter. You'll drive me mad, her mother said to him, and indeed it seems he had. Her mother was released for a short while. She spent her first day back looking through a trunk, something even sane people do at times. In this instance she was searching for ammunition to fire her mind for further anguish. Her daughter made tea three times and tried to keep her warm.

"Don't fuss around me like that. Don't do it, missy."

That word missy came and went like a whip. The welts it raised stung on a daily basis. The home was three counties off. (Asylum, poor farm, it is all the same.) The doctor, in a sagacious mood, implied that the change of life takes some ladies this way. They get over it, he said. Max did not want to think about it, having not long before been introduced to the first change herself.

Her uncle went because he had to sign the papers. There was no joy in her return because she could scald the hide from him with little effort. A half-dozen words could do it smartly. Her mother did not mean it unkindly. It might do him some good after all. That was not likely but the reproaches this time quickly ceased. Max's mother said little at first and then, soon, she said even less. She wouldn't eat and stopped using the privy. She made clear what she wanted without speaking. They hosed her down in the yard so she would be fit for the bus and went back the same way again. Max's mother had become used to quiet repetition and on Sundays there was vanilla ice cream for dessert.

She called the mare Max though no one else did. The mare was a gray Percheron and lived for toil. Max did not like her own given name, which was girly and had too many syllables. It derived from a flight of fancy on her mother's part, a last fling before the farm closed in on her again. Max did everything a girl was expected to do the year round but reserved her special indulgence for the mare.

The name Max probably came from the radio. They had one at the general store and if she had a nickel for a Baby Ruth she sometimes heard jokes about Jack Benny's Maxwell automobile or the Maxwell House coffee advertisements. She told her mother once what she heard.

"They say that coffee is good to the last drop," she said.

Her mother told her not to get her hopes up because nothing was. Go ahead, she added, ask the man being hanged how he feels about the last drop. Her mother had her own brand of playfulness.

Max assumed Maxwell was only a company name like Ford or McCormick and therefore suitable for adoption. The mare liked to have its ears scratched and seemed to enjoy being called Maxwell. This was eventually shortened to Max from a simple desire for closeness.

There are people who like a hearth but Max looked into that horse's eye and felt warmth brimming inside. She used the milking stool to climb on the mare and once fell asleep with her head on its neck. She brought it carrots and turnips. They were like most of the farm and its progeny, ill begotten, though the mare was not so discriminating. The mare understood who groomed her, who covered her in her stall, and who treated the bit sores around her mouth. The barn nuzzles Max received as recompense followed her on the cold pathways to the house.

Her uncle, strangely enough, was afraid of horses though the man he most esteemed, more strangely perhaps, was the farrier.

The farrier went all over, a gypsy rover, no flies on him, exuding an independence, a dominance that reduced her uncle, not eloquent to begin with, to speechlessness.

The farrier was said to have patriarchal tendencies, having provided his services when hard money or trade goods were not present. He'd learned some things in France during the war (he was an army mule skinner) that took but a minute or two and if they looked on the beasts of the field did not object. He did leave a child or two in his backwash, when someone's ardor flagged him down, but it is a forgiving country for the most part where everyone looks like everyone else.

Max's uncle was not a man comfortable with debt. Lincoln's people had moved up from Kentucky because Indiana was free soil. Her uncle had learned this in his schoolhouse days and believed it was so until his own bondage began. He was in harness and could not say with Abraham that the judgments of the Lord are true and righteous altogether.

The farrier did not appear to age. It's being out in the open air, he explained, footloose, unencumbered. Her uncle nodded, no stranger at least to the open air. Money was owing for shoeings. There had been equine influenza about and the farrier was doing a little horse trading to help out. It was cash in hand and the mare was gone before her uncle was done counting it. The farrier was sure of himself and had brought a horse carrier with him.

"You want to eat, don't you?"

Max wasn't sure she did. She'd seen the farrier, for whom she had an instinctual dislike, take the mare and decided the solitary food she ate was not a fair exchange. In any case the store bought food would not last and there they would be again. Her uncle did not drink and he did not chew and he did not swear. He was a good man who could not raise a crop or make a decision he did not regret. He whistled well though there was seldom a reason for it.

There were a few not very useful skills. In one of her final rages, her mother knocked a picture from the wall in what they called the best room. It was a Winslow Homer reproduction Max received for reciting "John Brown's Body" without undue hesitation at school. She was not the best, she was the poorest, and it was third prize. The first two prizes were a five dollar bill and a two dollar bill.

A man stands in a field holding a scythe. He has stopped working to listen to the call of a bird. The painting seemed emblematic of her uncle but he repaired the frame without comment. The few paintings Max had seen, in mail order catalogs, were intended to tell a story. She understood what Winslow Homer intended. It was plain enough to her but whether the man in the field continues reaping or goes on to follow the song of the lark she could not for the moment determine. He might, she supposed, walk out of the frame into another world. There is so much that comes out of nowhere.

After her uncle repaired the picture she nailed it above her bed. She had never slept anywhere else. Along with her other desires she dreamed about it at night. Every morning she said the same thing though it no longer had to do with the man in the field. The first chance she had she would call herself Max and no one would ever sell her.

2005

There were voices above Salome's head. It was not the first time. If it was not cold she left the door of the Silvercup van open as she slept. (The stench of the cats was strong but they had long preceded her. There was a new litter as well.) During the night she was feverish and there was an ache in her inner ear. (Salome was allergic to penicillin though this was never established. She suffered from repeated ear aches as a child.)

The cough she'd had all of the winter was stronger and there was spittle on the oven mitts she wore to bed. (Her sleeping bag had been stolen. She wrapped herself in a cat-clawed moving blanket and newspapers.) There was laughter. The voices broke up, resumed, and broke up again as the procession of planners and architects moved at a window shopping pace from the Nabisco Building to Gansevoort Street. The media coverage was more than anyone had expected.

A metro page reporter made a wet snowball and hit, rather expertly, the Z of ZWERLING on the building wall. (It was early April snow, not meant to last.) The entrances were bricked up.

Good packing, he called out, wanting to be boyish. There was no antiphon. He suspected there was not a true New Yorker in the bunch.

A photographer stumbled over the nearly invisible train tracks, dropping his light meter. He swore, a little embarrassed by the word he used. He disliked reaching his arm into all that growth. There might be snakes. There was a rusted tool of some kind, one of those curved things farmers used to use. He did not want tetanus. (He was free lance and did not have health insurance.)

The lavish groundcover Salome engendered was now unchecked, no longer tended by her. Nature had resumed its furious conquest, awaiting her rebirth. She slept many hours of the day, cut off at the root, disinherited.

"Is that bamboo? Will that grow here?"

Some of the group were women, concerned about their shoes and stockings. (They walked gingerly, getting a good whiff of cats. Heat rises and curiously so does stink.) The reporter had his eye on the one from the mayor's office. He'd seen her in the press office at City Hall with teeth that could bite through the Zagat guide. Today she possessed the highest heels on the platform of the scissor lift. (The mayor had more money than God and liked them dressy.) Their ascent to the viaduct had her squealing.

"Whee...this is super."

The reporter threw another snowball, unable to agree. What are you supposed to say about a new park thirty feet in the air where you couldn't jog or play softball? You said what everyone hopes to hear about urban revival or whatever they call it now.

You don't say it was more Mickey Mouse for MBA's and their handmaidens and tourists clogging the streets. Manhattan was getting as bad as Venice in his estimation.

The reporter looked over the side of the viaduct. Gloveless, the iron felt like cold monkey bars on his hands, back around Ditmars Boulevard. It went through him like that Silvercup van down there. (As a child, standing on the Queens Plaza station, he'd smelled the bread baking, drifting from the Silvercup sign, the Parthenon of Long Island City, his temple of Athena.)

And now the goddamn Whitney, they say, wants to come down here and shove Piss Christ in everyone's face. (The Whitney would also bring the mid-century portrait of Max when she was pregnant. As the reporter watched, that former embryo emerged from the van, frightened, needing to pee, fumbling for the bucket she squatted on.)

There was a carcass of some kind under the blackened leaves and the reporter shoved it away with his shoe. The group had moved on. They were talking about eating.

"Are you coming?"

The reporter supposed so. He looked again. The woman below him was urinating into a mud bucket outside a building with a demolition notice on it. She was gray haired, stooping as she stood, pulling up her pants. A heck of a mustache too. She rubbed snow between her fingers. That needs a painter, the reporter granted. He didn't have the words for it.

Three years had passed since the hardware store was condemned. The front and back doors were cinderblocked and arcane Department of Buildings signs were chalked on the sidewalk. Salome did not know what they meant. (Because of the leaking roof she had some time before brought her mattress downstairs to the Silvercup van. Whenever possible she'd stay on the viaduct. But that was no more.)

Before the building was shut up she went to the basement at times to look for something to sell. There was little left. She was in the basement when the workmen arrived. (She was afraid they might be the same ones who broke open the walls. The ones who tore out the copper piping and cursed so loud she crouched under Emmett's old bed.)

In a corner she'd found one of Mr. Zwerling's toys. It was a cat whisker telegraph key he played with at the counter. He liked to fix things and explained what he was doing to her. She understood him though he covered his mouth when he spoke.

Those workmen had brought a cement mixer. The noise brought her up from the basement. She came out the back door and saw them at the gate, bringing in their tools. She hid in the Silvercup van, her heart beating fast. They sealed the building and ripped down the wooden staircase. She remembered this so often. She went the wrong way. If she had been a little quicker she might have got up the staircase to the loft before them. She might have got on the roof ahead of them. This was her expulsion. She might have crossed over. She would be on the viaduct still and living off the land. All that remained of it was under her fingernails.

The Square Meal was served with an eviction notice. The restaurant opened the year Roosevelt came in and was a one story taxpayer on a vacant lot. (Drivers stalled on West Street smelled breakfast from the exhaust fans and felt like stopping.) The dollar bills taped to the side of the cash register were Silver Certificates. There were two. A third one was pulled off by a young man with an overwhelming morning jones like being squeezed in a vise. (A coin and stamp dealer gave him three bucks for it to get him out of the store.)

Alphonse accepted this theft as a sign the ax was coming soon. For most of its lifetime the Square Meal opened at two in the morning and closed at two in the afternoon. The meat packers ate there as well as cops and taxi drivers. There were six stools and four booths and a coat tree with a raincoat that was left on it in 1958.

"I don't know, he might come back."

When the Cunard ships docked at Pier 54 the darndest people used to come in. Hollywood royalty and gangsters and Hemingway one time right after the war with a new wife. (This was in truth his father speaking, speaking through him like a medium. Alphonse grew up helping out. He adopted his father's counter talk, partially in recompense for breaking his heart by marrying a girl from the Sailor's Rest with almond colored eyes. He told Max this one day, he could not say why. She was a good listener. Max kept it to herself. Mr. Zwerling knew the story too and was likewise mum about it.)

"I had guys in tuxedos and stuff sitting right where you are. I'm telling you. And the chauffeurs. They'd get in a card game waiting for the ship to come in. Right where you're sitting. No kidding."

That was long past. And after years of being other things, the Sailor's Rest was devoted to girls again. (A great disease, something like a plague, had scoured the young men away a generation earlier. Alphonse sold a good amount of coffee and danish to them when the bars closed for the night. He called cabs and cashed the odd check. It's good to be called Al. It's easy to remember.) The new girls were different but just the same. They sat in the booths and looked at the snow and then at the rain and then at the wavy heat. They did piecework like other immigrants used to do.

"Not a good life for anybody."

Alphonse never begrudged a single person sitting at a booth. Sometimes people need that and what can you say. That's why you have booths. In all fairness, familiar faces were a pleasure and there were not so many any more that he could choose to be choosy.

Another indication (the writing on the wall once again) came when the planners and architects stopped in for local color and brunch. (When it came to a western omelet, the Square Meal was first in show. The trick was said to be extra egg yolks and a trace of anchovy.) They filled the booths and stools and some stood. (One man declined to hang up his Aquascutum next to the raincoat on the coat tree. That raincoat looked contagious.)

The metro reporter asked Alphonse if he'd heard about the Whitney museum taking his little corner of paradise as their new playground. (Though native to the city, the reporter did not care for greasy spoons. Yet, as all concur, you could not beat them for home fries.)

It was news to Alphonse but he had nothing against museums. They were good for kids on a rainy day. (Like his daughter before she died wanting to see the big whale in the one uptown somewhere.) Alphonse did not wish to be picturesque, a grump in the newspaper. He wore a clean apron and washed his hands and had no gripe with nobody.

The reporter was disappointed. He needed a hook but this dime store philosophy lacked punch. He wanted a good lead the way he wanted in the mayoral assistant's leopard skin thong (he could well picture that) and perhaps the two were connected. So much was. That was no Bazooka wrapper on her left ring finger, he thought, but there was nothing three Negronis could not manage these days. He wondered where she lived.

Alphonse stared straight ahead above his booths and through his window to the street. He wasn't listening. The Salvation Army had sent him a dishwasher. The man had the shakes so bad he could not tie his shoelaces. (The drunk tank provides plastic slip-ons. They reminded Alphonse of patent leather and weddings.) The dishwasher's face was distorted. That's agony, ditto the boy who stole the dollar bill. It's all lopsided. The city was two kids on a seesaw and one was succulent like a pork roast and the other was not. (One gets the scraps, the bible says, one the back of the hand.)

Outside the window Alphonse saw Salome passing. She wandered, a little shaky. She was a mover in her own way. Her teeth were bad. He filled a coffee cup with egg salad and put it aside for her. She could mush that. The mother would never say no to a jelly doughnut for that little girl.

"That one, that was Max. Always had time to talk. She never gave a living soul the high hat that I know of. That's good. Know what I mean?"

Alphonse went on to say that nothing lasts, that's how it was, nothing you can do about it. The reporter turned away, still dissatisfied. The mayor's assistant asked for a Perrier in a clean glass.

The reporter had his limits. "Why not ask for the wine list while you're at it? Something to pair with the meatloaf."

She did not like his tone of voice. "Screw you," she said.

Salome had a very good D'Agostino shopping cart, almost new. It did not wobble like her last one. The cart easily held two compactor bags of the bottles and cans she collected. She took them to Eleventh Avenue but that transfer station was moving to Brooklyn. They told her no more after September. The summer was easier on the body though there were flies and her hands were often sticky. The Burger King got mad when you waited for the bathroom door to open. They chased her. The Au Bon Pain (she could not imagine how to say it) was good until someone complained. They had nice soap.

The mumbling did not help. It bothers people when you mumble and you have a do rag on your speckled head. You mumble and they move away. She tried not to. Sometimes Max spoke to her and she could not help it. When she heard Max she was happy. They had a lot to talk about.

The windows of the Square Meal were whitewashed. Salome looked in the rolloff but there was nothing left. On

the restaurant's last day the remaining food was dumped outside. She filled her shopping cart and wheeled it up to the
Silvercup van.

The cats ate ham and salami and chicken salad. There was
a box of hot cross buns. The food made her a little lazy and she
did not go out for three days except to use the bucket. The cats
were content and slept more and did not fight. One was less
feral than it used to be and crept under the moving blanket
with her. They both snored though Salome often woke for no
reason that she knew. Late at night when it was quieter she
heard an osprey returning with food for its young. She was
growing deaf.

Up Tenth Avenue this day, Salome saw the trucks. There was
also a crane. They had arrived since she'd left in the morning.
Some of the girls had come out of the Sailor's Rest to watch
from the street. Two others looked out of their windows. It was
a diversion at least.

Salome stopped, holding onto the handle of her shopping
cart. A portion of the building was down. The hydraulic arm of
the excavator hit the upper floor again and sections of masonry
and plaster were pulled out by the crusher. The light was good
and on the next swing of the hydraulic arm she saw the pink and
yellow and orange fragments of the Dutch Boy fresco fluttering.
They scattered over and onto the sidewalk. Salome pushed her
cart forward, attempting to squeeze between the sawhorses. A
man in a hard hat put out his hand.

"Don't be crazy," he said.

The hydraulic arm came down on the HARDWARE sign and collapsed the frame of the front door. They stopped to begin hauling debris. A tow truck dragged the Silvercup van from the side yard. Cats scrambled from underneath it. Salome looked left and right, not understanding. She could not take in what this meant. Above her there was a backhoe on the viaduct. It struggled over the tracks, scooping at fill. The backhoe cut a rabbit in half and its blade cracked the plywood base of the osprey stand. Two birds rose up from the splintering, stunned and screeching, leaving a chick behind. Salome thrust out her arms over her head, trying to follow. She felt them torn from her. The man in the hard hat pushed her back, reaching for his phone. The birds went higher, righting themselves. There was an updraft as Salome fell under the sawhorse, hitting her head on the curb. The birds went higher still, circling tip to tip over the deserted piers, beating on, beating on, bearing her lost covenant with life, her transit on this earth, across the Hudson and away.

NYC 2021